Corporeality

Stories

Corporeality

Stories

BY

Hollis Seamon

ABLE MUSE PRESS

Able Muse Press

www.ablemusepress.com

Printed in the United States of America

Library of Congress Control Number: 2012946632

ISBN 978-1-927409-03-9

Cover image: *Girl and Duck* by Renée Hoekzema

Cover & book design by Alexander Pepple

Able Muse Press is an imprint of *Able Muse:* A Review of Poetry, Prose & Art—at
www.ablemuse.com

Able Muse Press
467 Saratoga Avenue #602
San Jose, CA 95129

For my sons:

Tobias and Jacob Seamon

Having a body is not altogether serious.

Margaret Atwood, "Alien Territory," *Good Bones and Simple Murders*

Acknowledgments

I am grateful to the editors of the following journals where many of these stories originally appeared, often in different versions.

Bellevue Literary Review: "SUTHY Syndrome"

"The Plagiarist"

The Nebraska Review: "Annus Mirabilis"

The Greensboro Review: "Leave It Lie"

Fiction International: "Like a Virus"

Persimmon Tree: "The Trojan Cat"

Thanks to editor Danielle Ofri for reprinting "The Plagiarist" in *The Best of the Bellevue Literary Review.*

CONTENTS

3   SUTHY Syndrome

19   Annus Mirabilis

      19   Happily Ever After
      22   Once Upon a Time
      25   The Web Tangles
      29   Prince Charming
      32   The Wolf
      36   Fate
      38   Into the Dark
      40   Heroes: Blind, Beat and Bottled
      43   Happily Ever After, Again
      44   The End

45   Leave It Lie

67   Fatty Lumpkin vs. The Reaper:
Rounds One, Two and Three

      68   One
      77   Two
      80   Fatty hangs on
      82   Three

89 Gigantina

90   Growing (Way) Up
93   Taking a Lover (or Two)
96   Dying (Fairly) Young

103 The Plagiarist

123 Like a Virus

123   I. Paranoid Schizophrenia
127   II. Agoraphobia, Squared
136   III. Bats

141 The Trojan Cat:
A Drama in Three Acts

141   I
143   II
145   III

149 Praise Be to an Afflicting God

175 Cabbage Night

Corporeality

Stories

SUTHY Syndrome

I SHIT YOU NOT: RIGHT IN FRONT of the elevator that spits you into our hospice unit, there is—get ready for this—a harpist. This old lady with white hair and a weird long skirt sits by a honking huge wooden harp and strums. Or plucks, whatever. The harp makes all these sappy-sweet notes that glom themselves right onto your chest, no matter how hard you try to keep them off.

How sick is that? I mean, isn't that like a bit premature? I sit there in my wheelchair, on good days, and I just watch people get off the elevator. They're here to visit their dying whoevers and they think, just for a second, that they've skipped right over the whole death and funeral mess and gone straight to heaven. You think they'd be pleased, right? But no. Let me tell you, those visitors don't like it a bit. Most of them actually back up and some of them press the elevator button, trying to escape. Because, after all, *they're* not the ones dying, right? So why are *they* here? How did *they* end up in harp-land? It freaks them right out and I laugh my ass off. The counselors, and believe me the place is crawling with them, they tell me that harp music is soothing and spiritual and good for the patients. Okay, I say, fine. Maybe for the 95% of the patients that are ancient, like sixty and above, it's good. But what about for me? Or Sylvie? Me and Sylvie, I say, we're *kids*. We're fucking *teenagers* and we're dying, too, and what about *our* rights?

Okay, that's kind of mean, I admit. Because the counselors really are sort of cool and they get all teary when I say that because no one, and I mean no one, wants to think of kids dying. But we are, so I say, deal with it.

Anyway, this is what me and Sylvie did, one of the days when she was feeling decent enough to get up. Listen to this—it was a riot. We waited until around 5:30 p.m., when all of those long-faced loved ones always show up, and we went to the lobby and moved right into the harpy's space—I know, I know—harpy's a pun, folks, that's what me and Sylvie call her—and we covered up the elevator button with a big black arrow pointing down and we sat in our chairs, with, like, insane death-mask makeup on our faces—pale green with big black circles drawn around our eyes and streaks of red blood dripping from our lips—and we had my collector's item Black Sabbath tee shirts over our clothes and Sylvie—it surprised me that she had the energy—she had made a big red devil fork thing out of an IV pole—I think she actually painted the whole thing with nail polish, I mean a real project—and she was holding onto that. And I'd put one of my uncle's rave tapes—all screaming cool distortion—into the CD player and we blasted that sucker. I held up my handmade sign—***GOING DOWN—THIS MEANS YOU!***—written in fake flames and we both did, honestly, cackle and screech like insane demons. Okay, so it was just a joke, but Sylvie—that girl is much tougher than you'd think, given she's about five feet nothing, all shrunk up and bald—she took it maybe an inch too far when she pulled out a lighter and a box of Kleenex—you know, those cheesy cardboard ones they always give you in hospitals, peel the skin right off your nose?—and she lit those babies up and threw them on the floor. Made great flames, for about one millisecond.

Then all hell—ha, ha—really did break loose. Nurses and doctors and custodians and volunteers and counselors and probably the priests and the rabbis, too—there are always about six guys in black wandering our halls—they all came running and shouting and about nine thousand feet stomped out that one little fire. And me and Sylvie, we laughed our asses off, even when they started yelling at us and telling us to go back to our rooms and not come out again. And that was pretty funny, too—sending us to our rooms like little kids. Some punishment. I mean, what were they going to do to us, kill us? Sentence us to death? Hee, hee, hee.

The best part, for me, was when some visitor—well, not just some visitor, Mrs. Elkins's son, I actually know him, I play gin rummy with him in the visitor's lounge when the nights are long, as in, when aren't the nights here long?—grabbed me by the arm and screamed in my face: "What's the *matter* with you, Richie? Where's your respect? What's the *matter* with you?"

And I got to say one of my favorite lines, the one I pull out umpteen times a day, whenever some new priest/therapist/rabbi/ nurse/intern/visitor/whoeverthefuck asks me what's wrong with me. They can't ever seem to quite get it: obviously, I'm way too young to be here, so what's the story? They go: "Why are you here? What's *wrong* with you, son?" And that's when I always say— straight face, big innocent eyes—"I have SUTHY Syndrome." And when they go all blank and say, essentially, "Huh?" I get to say it again. "SUTHY syndrome. It's an acronym." Some of the dumbfucks don't even know what that means, but I always wait a beat and then spell it out: "I've got the Somebody Up There Hates You syndrome."

And, you know, really, it's a pretty good diagnosis, don't you think? For me, for Sylvie, for all the way-under-sixties that end up here and places like it, usually after what our obituaries will soon call a "courageous battle with fill-in-the-blank." How else you going to account for us? Hell, somebody up there hates us and that's that. SUTHY is the only answer that makes any damn sense.

ANYWAY, THAT WAS the last day Sylvie came out of her room. I think it took a lot out of her. Shit, at least she got to get in trouble, though, like any other kid. Her father bawled her out for like an hour. That man has a temper. But Sylvie got to wear makeup, too, and that was a real plus. I know she likes makeup. She's a girl, you know, even if she looks like some Halloween joke, now, all the time. I can see it, a little, the girl under the mask. Sometimes.

THERE'S THIS OTHER thing that happened between me and Sylvie, about a week after our Devil's Night event. This thing—which I promised her I'd never talk about to anyone and who the hell am I going to tell anyway?—had to do with virginity. I'm aware—not usually a hot topic around hospice, but for me and Sylvie, yeah. Kind of key. Anyway, I had rolled into her room one day and she whispered through the steel railing on her bed—"Richie, please, I don't want to die a virgin"—so soft I almost missed it. But, hell, you have to talk soft because there's absolutely not one fucking iota of privacy in this place. I mean, at home, we'd have KEEP OUT signs on our bedroom doors and all of that shit, but here? Here, Sylvie's mother and three little brothers hang around her room all day—the little ones play with matchbox cars under her bed and the biggest one sits in a corner with comic books and her mother hovers nonstop, all red-eyed and swollen-faced. Once, I heard Sylvie yell at her mother, who'd asked her something simple, like, "Do you want another blanket, honey?" Sylvie sat up in bed like a screaming banshee and wailed: "No, I don't. I want to be left alone. Leave me the hell aloooooooooooooooooooone." Swear to God, that last syllable went on for like twenty seconds. Then her mother—short little dark-haired Italian lady, all round and soft—and the three little boys scooted their asses out of there. Then I heard Sylvie crying in her bed, saying "Shit, shit, shit, shit, shit." And so I didn't go in, that afternoon. And the mother and boys didn't come back that night. No, that night—and every one after that—it's Sylvie's father who camps on the cot in her room. And, believe me, that man scares the bejesus out of me. That man is so mad, so furious and so sad and so, I don't know even how to say it, so like fucking nuclear-blasted by his daughter dying that he gives off toxic fumes. Swear to God, the man glows orange and he hates everybody and, once, he was escorted off the floor by two big security guys after taking a swing at a nurse—a male nurse, okay, so that's not so bad—and they only let him back on when some therapist assured everyone he'd settled down. Settled down? Ha. That guy won't settle, ever again, I figure. He'll be batshit mad for life. His little girl gets a death sentence and he gets a life sentence. Sweet, huh? SUTHY, I'm telling you.

And that's another thing that drives me crazy here. Families. Back in the regular hospitals—where, believe me, I've done my time, over and over, repeat offender—they kind of keep check on how many family members can show up at one time and bother the shit out of you and so on, so you get a little time off. (Except for the Puerto Rican families in the big hospital in the city. Man, no one could keep those people out: grandpas, great-grand-somethings, seventeen aunts with three or four kids each, never mind the parents—everyone carrying some kind of food in an aluminum container, smelled like garlic and onion and spice—the whole *familia* showing up day and night. Kind of fun, now that I remember it. And best damn meals I ever had, whenever my roommate was PR or Dominican or some other kind of Spanish dude. Good times, actually.) But, here, no. There ain't no big rules about visiting hours and shit. Here they say they're "treating the whole family." So it's like, mad crowded, in some rooms. But some rooms—and maybe this is worse—are empty. Where some nine-hundred-year-old somebody who looks like a mummy already is dying all alone. That's sort of sad, to me. So sometimes I roll in and stay a few minutes with the old guy or woman, sort of pat their hands. Whatever.

My room, by the way, isn't full of folks but isn't totally empty, either. My uncle came here once. Cried and left after about three minutes, but, shit, he showed up, right? And my mom comes in late every night and sleeps on a cot. She's got to keep working, so she's not here all day. And before anyone thinks, Man, what a cold mother, let me tell you something. My mom had me when she was my age, exactly, seventeen. And there's only us and she works two jobs and she keeps us in health insurance and if you think that's been easy, if you think she doesn't care, if you think her heart isn't torn into little tiny shreds, you can go fuck yourself. My mom is here nights and she looks sicker than me and she shakes and cries and has to go out for a smoke and when she comes back in, I let her kiss me, just so I can taste tobacco, and then she falls asleep and I look at her curled up on that crappy cot, her cheeks all sunk in and her eyes all puffy, and I think I'm going to lose it. And sometimes I do, the only time, the only fucking time the sadness comes through and I want to kill anybody who hurts her and, yes, I'm aware that there is nobody else on earth who could hurt her like I am doing, right now. And that is the last I'll say about my mom. That's the one thing I can't talk about. So don't ask.

So, OKAY, BACK to Sylvie and me and our "date." Of course, to be honest, at home, a girl like Sylvie used to be wouldn't look twice at a guy like I used to be. I mean, I've seen the pictures of her that her mom's got plastered all over the walls of her room: Sylvie on the swim team—all long legs and nice round boobs in a stretchy suit; Sylvie going to her junior high prom in a pink gown; Sylvie as a brown-eyed, black-haired baby; Sylvie with a bunch of friends, all the boys tall and handsome; Sylvie on the front porch of a big white house, her baby brothers on her lap; Sylvie, tan and glowing; Sylvie, Sylvie, Sylvie. So you know that somewhere inside this yellow-skinned, bag-of-bones, bald-headed Sylvie, there's that other one: cool, popular, smart. And inside the ditto-ditto-ditto Richie, there's the kid-raised-by-a-single-mother-on-about-three-cents-a-month, not-so-cute, mouthy-and-smart-but-not-even-half-popular kid doomed to walk ten paces behind the Sylvie-type girl, mooning and yearning, who never once gets up his nerve to speak. Never happen. (Yeah, my mom has one picture of me, taped above my bed. I'm seven years old and wearing my little league uniform. Says Ajax Hardware across my chest. My cap is about five sizes too big and I have no front teeth. Makes me cringe, but Mom likes it, so what the hell.)

But here in hospice, miracles do happen. As in, the once-beautiful Sylvie asks the once-and-always-dorky Richie to help her get over her virginity. Hell, maybe dying's not so bad, hey?

So, okay, I'm a little nervous. I prepare a few witty lines to say, just in case. Because, hey, I'm not so one hundred percent sure that I can even do it. I mean, come on, man. I'm not exactly in tip-top condition here. Anyway, I wait until Sylvie's first-shift guardians go home—her mother stopping in the hallway to cry for like twenty minutes and the little bros all sucking their thumbs, looking totally lost—and her second-shift hasn't yet shown up. Her dad usually blasts into the place around seven p.m. So, it's like 6 when I wheel myself into Sylvie's room. Here's what it's like: big window that looks out over the city of Hudson and, way off down the hill, the river. Great view, except that Sylvie can't sit up anymore to see it. One bed. No tubes or monitors or anything. That's the one good thing. In hospice, they stop torturing you. No more burning the shit out of you with radiation. No more chemo poison into the veins. No more puking, no more physical therapy, no more poking and prodding and telling you to fight to get better. Think positive. Like it's all in your head. Like your fucking *attitude* counts. No more. Because if this was a battle, hey, dude, you lost. So, for a booby prize, they let you eat if you want (I don't want); they give you whatever dope you ask for; they let you sleep; they're all sort of gentle and kind. So here Sylvie is, in the bed, covered with a quilt that her mother and her aunts all made, by hand, with bits and pieces of, I swear, Sylvie's baby clothes and shit—all pink and fluffy and soft. Sylvie told me, once, that she nearly pukes every time she looks at it. She wanted, she said, black Polartec with a picture of a wolf on it, howling at the moon. Right now, she's curled into a ball and she's asleep—or at least her eyes are closed. Light hurts our eyes, did you know that? That when you're this far gone, you want to see sunlight and all, but it hurts. You're heading for the dark, that's what that means. (I'm not going to go into what we feel like because it's just so boring. Just this one thing—it's like being hollowed out. Like, I don't know, a cantaloupe or something, after your spoon's been in there scraping. It's all shell, man, with the last little bit of juice leaking out.)

I don't know what to do about Sylvie and the bed and the virginity and all. I mean, what's the etiquette here? I'm here to take care of business, I understand that, but I don't think I can just crawl into bed with the girl. And I'm getting scared, you know? I mean, I'm what you'd call new to this whole thing, too. Didn't ever, not even once, convince some kindhearted pretty nurse to give a guy a parting gift. Tried. Failed. Okay, so I'm about to back the chair out of the room, just roll off into the sunset, when Sylvie opens her eyes. They were, you can tell from the pictures, some of the darkest, biggest, brownest eyes you ever saw. All fringed with black eyelashes and all. Now, they're bald and red-rimmed like—I hate to say it, but like reptile eyes. But there's still some spark there, you know. Because Sylvie winks one eye and says, "No escape, Richard. Get your ass up here." And she moves over in the bed—I mean, there's like room for three Sylvies and two mes in that bed—and pats the sheet.

So I get up out of the chair—and, I can't lie, that takes me some time. My legs ain't what they used to be. I sort of winch myself up onto the bed and I slide under the quilt. We lie eye-to-eye, just kind of staring at each other. I want to lighten things up and so I bring out one of my preprepared lines. "Should I wear a condom, prevent us from getting some awful disease?" I say.

And, same exact minute, we both start to laugh. I mean, funny just doesn't describe it: two, bald-headed, wrinkled-up raisins, we just lose it. We laugh until our faces hurt. And we giggle for a long while after that. So that makes all the rest okay. I can touch her now—her little bird-bones and her skin so fragile that it'll tear if I'm not careful. And I can kiss her—our cracked dry lips give it a try, anyway. And I can hold her tiny breasts in the palms of my hands. And that's all I'm going to say. My mama raised a gentleman. But, okay, here's a hint: it wasn't exactly totally successful and I guess that we'll both die virgins, technically. But, hey, we gave it a shot. And it was worth it, just for that long, sweet laugh. That's all I'm saying.

Oh, except for one semi-creepy thing. I'm pretty sure that sometime in there, while me and Sylvie were sort of sleepy and nodding off together in her bed, her father was in the room. I mean, I'm not one hundred percent certain, because if he was, wouldn't you think he'd have dragged my naked ass out of bed? Kicked my butt from here to eternity? Nope, nothing like that happened. But there was a smell of bourbon in the room, for a minute, and Wild Turkey is Sylvie's dad's painkiller of choice. And, as I've mentioned, there ain't no locks on these friggin' doors. But, if he was there, he didn't do a damn thing and when I left, he was just sitting at the nurses' station, not even bothering them. Just sitting there. Looking into space.

COUPLE DAYS AFTER THAT, Sylvie stops talking and she doesn't open her eyes or her mouth, except to sip water. Her little brothers come back only once and each one of them leaves one thing on the end of her bed: one red car, one blue car and one DC comic. Her parents come in together and they never leave. Once, I see my mother go into that room and Sylvie's mom and my mom hold onto each other like the Titanic is sinking under their feet, like ice-cold water is up to their armpits, rising fast. They rock, swaying together. And they fucking wail. You never heard such a thing in your life. Hope you never do. It damn near kills me and I start asking for a whole lot more morphine, not that I have that much pain—I don't anymore—but I just want to go to sleep and not hear anything, ever again.

Once, though, when I'm sleeping, all fogged up with drugs, the harpy sneaks into my room, swear to God, and plays that goddamn angel music. I'm so stoned I haven't got the strength to tell her to shut up. And that music gets into my chest and it makes me cry, right there in the middle of my swirly dope-dreams. I'm crying and crying, in my dreams, and I can't stop and I'm blubbering like a two-year-old and I hate this fucking shit and I can't stop.

And that makes me so scared that I stop asking for the drugs. I decide to see it out, eyes open. Yeah, to be honest, I'm scared to sleep.

So I'm pretty alert for the last big event on our floor. I'm up and conscious at something like three a.m. Down the hall somewhere, the harpy is at it—in some poor sucker's room, for the all-night last-watch thing. I'm just trying to read, even though the letters on the page are all blurry, just trying to close my ears to the music. Glad it's far away. I'm keeping my light on, pretend-reading. My mom, finally, she takes herself into the lounge to rest; she never could stand a light on when she's trying to sleep. Anyway, who'd have guessed it could happen, shit, Sylvie's father goes around and organizes a poker game. I mean, the man's face is like a skull, no sleep for days, but suddenly, he walks by and sees that I'm awake in my bed—I can't get out of it anymore—and he says, "Hey, you, Mr. Smart-ass. You up for some cards?" and I say, "Sure." I mean, it'll pass the time, right?

So the man rounds up a couple of other late-night waiting-around-for-someone-to-die folks and they all edge into my room and pull up plastic chairs around my bed: Mrs. Elkins's son, Sylvie's father and some old lady I don't really know, who I heard has been sitting with her twin sister. (Think about that—watching your twin die. That's got to be harsh.) It's kind of crazy but what the hell, right? And, it's Sylvie's dad who comes up with the stakes. You ready for this? No, you're not. You can't be—it's such a mad brilliant idea. What we're playing for, he says, is days. You can win—or lose—however many days of life, for yourself—they all look at me—or your mother or your twin sister or your daughter. Simple five card stud, nothing wild. Basic, hard-ass poker. And we're playing for days. I love it.

We have no chips so Sylvie's dad rustles around in my bedside table—during which I smell booze on his breath and the heat from his body almost knocks me out. Anyway, there's all kinds of crap in there and he pulls out some stuff. This is what we decide: little plastic pill cups are worth one day each. Small gauze pads, two days. Big gauze pads, three. That's it. No one even considers saying anything is worth, like, a week. That's too much. We just go simple. We take it, ha ha, one day at a time.

HERE'S THE THING about me and card games. I've always been lucky. (Yeah, yeah, I'm aware—lucky at cards, unlucky at love. Seems right on, for me.) I mean, ever since I was a kid. I was beating my mom at Go Fish when I was four, no kidding. So I am psyched and I'm sure I'm going to win myself a whole bunch of days. And that's not a joke. Because maybe in that last week that I win, some brilliant scientist geek will come up with the cure, right? Could happen. It'll be some South American jungle serpent venom drug, I know it. Only something made from snakes is going to work on SUTHY, I'm convinced.

Don't worry, I'm not going to bore you with the whole play-by-play thing. We're not doing some cheesy Texas Hold 'Em broadcast here. It's pretty standard poker and everyone's winning some, losing some. That old lady, I got to say, she's tough. Can't read a wrinkle on that face and she's dead serious—I can see that she wants to win her sister some time, for real. Mrs. Elkins's son, he's all half-assed about it—you can bet he's ready for his mother to check out and he's just passing some time here. But the one who's dead-ass scary is Sylvie's dad. I mean, he's not playing cards—he is in a fucking war. His skin is gray, he's got stubble sticking every which way out of his face, he smells like someone pissed Wild Turkey all over him. Couple of times, I catch him staring at me and I kind of shudder. I mean, the man is on fire. If you took an infrared picture, swear to God, there'd be little flames leaping off the guy's ears. So, yeah, if you really want to know, I get into this weirded-out mental state. I think Sylvie's dad is the devil and I think I'm playing for my soul. No joke. I'm sweating here.

By let's say five a.m., Mrs. Elkins's son has dropped. He's flat asleep in his chair, snoring like a chain saw. And the old lady, she started to curse, last hand when she drew nothing and she threw her cards onto the bed table and marched out the room, stamping her feet.

Hey, you could see this coming a mile away, right? Yep, it's down to Richie vs. The Devil. Try to get the whole picture: there's a harpy making creepy angel noises way off down the hall. Dawn's just coming into the sky outside. And there's a whole heap of days lying on the table between us and we're both out of anything to add to the pot. It's one of those moments, you know? And I'm looking at the three jacks I hold in my hand. All mine. Sweet. And he's looking at . . . who knows? Well, he's looking at me, that's all. He's waiting for it. He ain't got shit, I can tell. Here's the trick: it's not the eyes, like some people say, that give you away. It's the lips. Lips tremble, you know? When you really, really, absolutely, positively, no shit *have to win*, lips'll betray you. And Sylvie's dad—Mr. Lucifer, let's call him—his mouth looks like a pair of bat wings, all fluttery.

I look at the pot—I figure there're three weeks of life there. Maybe more. More than enough time for the scientist-dude to come through, right?

I've got the winning hand, no question. And I'm just about to lay it down and claim my days, when the man pulls a nasty trick. First, he lays down his hand, face up. He's got a pair of queens. Both dark-haired, dark-eyed ladies. Then he looks right into my eyes and he says, "She's fifteen, Richard."

In other words, I've already had two more years. I already lived something like seven hundred and thirty more days than Sylvie. I look at my three of a kind: Jack Spade, Jack Diamond, and Jack Heart. Two of them are those shifty one-eyed guys, little skinny mustaches, slicked-back hair, look like pimps. I think about Sylvie's tiny breasts, soft as baby birds in my hands. And I fold my cards up and put them down, their faces hidden. Doesn't matter, he's not going to look. Can't stand to look. Doesn't want to know. "You got me, sir," I say. "Congratulations."

Mr. Lucifer sweeps all the days into his arms. He's laughing like a hyena.

★ ★ ★

NEXT MORNING I HEAR THAT, overnight, two people died. Whoever the harpy was playing to and Mrs. Elkins. (I figure she hurried herself to get it done while her son was out of the room. No fuss, no bother.) But here's the cool thing: over that same night, Sylvie rallied. I hear from the morning nurse that Sylvie's sitting up and drinking coffee. That's what she asked for. Not water, not ginger ale—coffee. Black and hot. That's my girl. Maybe she'll grab her three weeks and walk on out of here. Maybe she'll get two years. Maybe forever. Shit, any way you look at it, me and Sylvie, we won.

Annus Mirabilis

W E'VE ALL OF US, HAVEN'T WE, wished for a year of miracles? A miraculous year?

Year of restoration, year of renewal, year of renaissance. Year of marvels, marvelous year.

Yeah, right. We won't get it, we know that. Not hardly. Fat chance. *As if!*

That's why there are fairy tales, eh?

So, yes: Once upon a time, Vivian Worth, quiet, plain, fortyish, and grouchy, had herself a miraculous year.

Well, all right, not quite. A miraculous three months. That's enough, anyway.

Enough and more than we'll ever get, that's for sure. Except in stories.

This one begins. . . .

Happily Ever After

D R. VIVIAN WORTH'S CAREER as a professor came to end at 6:15 on the night of September 19, 2000. The semester barely begun, the evening class just started. Apropos of absolutely nothing at all—the class had been discussing *The Odyssey*, the really good parts, Circe and the Cyclops and the pig-sailors—one of Vivian's students said, "Hey, you know what? Edmund Wilson's daughter had a really big head." (Well, okay, maybe this comment wasn't such a non sequitur, Vivian now considers. Maybe it had something to do with transformation, something to do with freakishness, something to do with magic. And the student, a woman of a certain age, had hung out, in her youth, with Ginsberg and Ferlinghetti and that crowd and had the photographs and autographed manuscripts to prove it. A true and surviving Beatwoman. Now that Vivian has the mental leisure to consider such things, she sees that this was a perfectly reasonable segue, really. Brilliant, actually. That Ginsberg would have said so—howled so—well, of that she's certain.)

Into the silence that befell the classroom, the Beatwoman laughed, happily. "And no neck. Really! I saw her once in a diner in San Francisco, Edmund Wilson's daughter. She was sitting in a booth, with this head like a—I don't know, a Macy's Parade balloon—and I went and looked closer and she had no neck. And a really round body." The Beatwoman settled back into her chair and sighed at the deliciousness of this memory. "Well," she added, "lots of bizarre people go to diners."

And that was that. Vivian dismissed the class. She had to shove some of them out of the room, they were so befuddled at being dismissed fifteen minutes into the period. But, really, what could one possibly say, after that? She simply couldn't get the image out of her head: Edmund Wilson's big-headed daughter, floating in the diner booth in the heart of beatnik Frisco, tied down by hidden ropes. Worse, for a few minutes, she confused Edmund Wilson with Gahan Wilson and the image got even stranger: the daughter became a huge-headed cartoon figure, drawn in Gahan

Wilson's shaky lines, face like a flattened hot-cross bun. Floating against the ceiling of the classroom, ropes all unfurled, hanging loose behind her. Bumping against the fluorescent lights, seeking egress through the high windows. Questing for the sky.

Well. You can imagine. It was over. Clearly. Vivian carried her *Norton Anthology of World Masterpieces* out of the building and left it on the outside stairs, shining in the sun of that fine September evening. She walked home, even though she'd left her car in the university lot. It wasn't that far—three, four miles. Light walking, without any books to carry.

She thought, all the way home, about Gahan/Edmund Wilson's daughter, with her big head. No neck. Round body. Her amazing lightness, her helium heart. She remembered that just that week, one of her colleagues had described her students as "cheeses with dial tones," a line from some poem or other. Vivian had misheard that, at first, thinking it was "Jesus with dial tones." And that image had been hard to shake, too, believe you me. Even when her colleague had clarified—"*Cheeses*, Viv. *Cheeses* with dial tones."—it only got worse. Vivian had seen her own students, for the rest of that day, as Camembert, Cheddar, Gouda. Brie. (One of the girls was *named* Brie, for goodness sake. What were parents thinking?) But, mostly, she saw the softer cheeses—unformed, slippery, squishy. Sometimes, Velveeta. But all the cheeses wore halos, sort of. Cheeses crowned in thorns. Cheeses on the cross.

So, maybe, Gahan/Edmund Wilson's daughter wasn't the whole problem, was she? Well, what do you think? Was she, that lovely round helium-head girl, the *whole* problem? Or was she, perhaps, the solution? The way to the happy ending? We shall see.

Once Upon a Time

VIVIAN'S SECOND CAREER BEGAN as soon as she got home on the night of September 19, 2000. But she didn't know it then. Then, it was just her normal evening reading session with the blind girl next door, the blind girl who played guitar in an up-and-coming local band. (The girl's name is Amanda and now her band is pretty famous, but it wasn't then. Now, when Amanda calls Viv, it's long distance, from airports in Amsterdam and Prague. Now, Amanda laughs, a tinny faraway laugh, and says, "They've never seen a blind white chick wail like me. They love me.") It wasn't until the next day—September 20, 2000—that Viv hung the sign on the front porch of her old Victorian house on Sea Street. (Vivian lives in a city situated four hundred miles from a sea of any kind; the name of her street is just one of its mysteries.) The sign read:

Bread* and Books
$10.00 per hour
Day or Night
(BYOB = Bring Your Own Book)
[*Homemade Bread]

But that night—September 19, 2000, remember?—which Vivian thought was an ending, not a beginning, she sat down as usual and waited for Amanda to come to the porch. She'd lit the lamp she kept on the front porch, hooked up to about twenty miles of orange extension cord, looped over the porch railings and snuggled under the fence, trailing over three backyards until it reached the one neighbor with an outdoor socket. She was early, since her class—and her career—was over. So she sat quietly, "The Dead" in her hands, listening to the crickets buzz. September crickets— Vivian wanted to cry just thinking about it, this last-ditch cricket-mating frenzy. Crickets crying out into the night—"Pick me! Let me be your mate! Let my DNA survive. Let me find immortality in the cricket gene pool. Oh please, oh please, oh pretty-pretty please, pick me!!!" Crickets who'd be dead, their little black cricket wings, their little black cricket legs, their big black cricket eyes all coated by frost, in about a week. (But—maybe not! Maybe crickets just hibernate for the winter!! Well, it's not impossible, is it? Nothing is really impossible, in stories.)

At 8:45, as usual, she heard Amanda's cane tapping out of the front door of the house next door, then, down her front walk. Amanda was the fastest blind-girl walker Viv had ever known; once, Viv had actually seen Amanda *run* for the University bus, charging down the sidewalk, cane bouncing in front of her, skipping just above the ground—amazing! The other people on the sidewalk that day—non-blind people—had fled the path of that adamant cane. So, here Amanda was, trucking on up Viv's front walk in double time: taptaptaptaptappitytaptap.

The late summer twilight—*very* late summer, equinox hanging just around the corner—and the orange glow of the city's crime lights, of course, lit the tip of Amanda's cane as it hopped happily along the old slates. Little bursts of light kept jumping up, as if the cane struck the slate like tinder, making sparks. (Now Viv knows that it did, it actually did spark, that Amanda's cane is capable of magic, capable of anything. But, then, it just looked nice.) By the time Amanda had plopped down on Viv's front steps,

Viv had the book open and she was reading from the paragraph where they'd left off, last night. It was one of her favorite bits: "A light fringe of snow lay like a cape on the shoulders of his overcoat and like toecaps on the toes of his galoshes; and, as the buttons of his overcoat slipped with a squeaking noise through the snow-stiffened frieze, a cold fragrant air from out-of-doors escaped from crevices and folds." (If you know the story, as you most certainly should, you realize that Viv and Amanda hadn't gotten very far in their reading. That's true. They didn't like to rush, even when Amanda had an exam coming up in her British literature class. They sometimes only got through a paragraph a night. Because, sometimes, the paragraph they'd just read broke both their hearts and, as you know, broken hearts take some time to set and mend.)

Amanda wriggled with happiness on the steps. "Oh, yes. I can smell it. I can hear it. Oh, man, that Joyce wrote for blind people! Oh man." Then she was quiet, waiting for the next line.

And Viv read it: "'—Is it snowing again, Mr. Conroy?' asked Lily." But then she had to stop, because tears were rising in her eyes and her throat was tight. You see, she *knew* what was coming—Gabriel Conroy's complacent heart to be pulled from his chest (metaphorically, of course) and coated by snows from the past, stories from the past, old snowy loves. Well, it's hard to keep reading when you know *that's* coming, isn't it? So Viv shut the book, and her eyes, and she and Amanda just sat there, silent and blind, smelling the snow and hearing the squeak of Gabriel's cold buttons above the crickets' cries. And it was only then that Viv *got* it, really. The whole idea of blindness—real and metaphoric. Only right that very minute, that she realized that Amanda couldn't *see*, for Christ sake. And never would. And never had. That the cold and the squeak were real, for Amanda, but not that lovely cape of snow, white across the shoulders of a black overcoat. Well, right then, Viv's heart broke for real. For Amanda. And, though she didn't know it then, that's what changed her life. She knows now, of course, that that's where the truest stories *begin*. With broken hearts.

The Web Tangles

VIVIAN DIDN'T SLEEP MUCH, the night of September 19, 2000. First, because her heart hurt. Actually ached, shuddering around in her chest like a hot nervous fist, beatingbeatingbeating. And second, because she was sorry she hadn't thanked the Beatwoman, for rescuing her. And, third, because there was a full moon, the Harvest Moon, shining in her window, laying its lunatic beams across her comforter. And, fourth, because she wished she'd gotten to thank Joyce, in person, for that snowy vision. And, fifth, because Amanda played her guitar, loud, most of the night, and the houses on Sea Street are very close together and neighbors can even hear each other breathe, on late-summer, open-window nights.

But sleeplessness isn't all bad. You can use it to plan, if you eschew bitterness and annoyance and just let yourself drift. And that's what Viv did—she floated all night on the crimelight-tinged moonbeams and *nouveau* Jimi Hendrix and by morning, she'd decided how to make her living in a way that would allow her heart to break and not stop it all up with objectivity and critical distance. (If you've ever been a professor of literature—or had a class with one—you know exactly what this feels like. You've felt your chest grow tight and your eyes fill up, with simple pity for Prufrock, say, walking the beach in his rolled-up trousers, looking desperately for a men's room on the sandy shore, because, that morning, he had dared to eat a peach, goddamn it. But you can't *say* so, can you? It's not allowed. You cannot speak your pity. Your simple stupid uncritical love. No. It is not allowed.) There were two things Vivian Worth could do, well. She could bake bread and she could read.

Thus, in the early morning light of September 20, 2000, the sign was hung over the porch railing. Then, a sunny happy morning was spent in the kitchen, immersed in flour and yeast and eggs. The phone rang, incessantly at first, less after a while. Her department chair, no doubt. Later, probably, the dean. Maybe even some students, concerned—Will I have to turn in my paper, Dr. Worth, if you don't come to class?

By about 3:15 that afternoon, three people were sitting on her porch, eating heavily buttered slices of homemade challah and listening to Vivian read aloud from *The Odyssey*. Yes, strangely enough, that's the very book the first man to arrive brought over. Of course it was—how couldn't it be? He was a street man; he wandered, especially on moonlit nights, catching the glitter of aluminum cans in gutters, the shine of green bottles in garbage cans. He'd wandered the campus, his most productive hunting grounds, where students toss off cans and bottles like snakes shedding skin, and he'd seen—Glory be!—*The Norton Anthology of World Masterpieces* sitting pretty on the step where Vivian's hand had dropped it. And it had, of course, fallen open to the page she'd last touched, and he'd started, very slowly at first, then with more speed, as his brain remembered—*remembered, imagine that!*—how to turn squiggles on a page into visions, to read. The Bottleman remembered how to read. Or maybe how to see, really. Because he saw, he actually saw, the Cyclops, hairy and one-eyed and stupid. He could, actually, smell the Cyclops (smelling something like himself, naturally, urine-stained and sweaty and crusted with cave-damp.) Yes, he saw and smelled them all. Circe. The poor doomed sailors. The Pig-men. Perfumed Penelope at her loom. All of them. Even Argos, good old faithful dog. Good dog, good dog.

Then, carrying the book, precious and heavy against his bare skin, under his stained shirt, he'd seen the sign on Vivian's porch and—well, he didn't have ten dollars, that's for sure, but Vivian had declared that the first day was free and so there they were, the Bottleman and the Old-Woman-Dressed-in-Suit-and-Pearls and the Schoolboy, sitting on the porch, being nourished. The Bottleman had brought his own faithful dog, a limping shepherd named Gesundheit; the Old-Woman-Dressed-in-Suit-and-Pearls had stopped by on her 19th trip of the day to the Price Chopper on the corner; the Schoolboy, shy, with skin as black as tar, stopped on his way home from the elementary school up the block.

Vivian, utterly delighted to find that the masterpieces of the world had found such a splendid new owner, started just where she'd left off with her class the night before. But they didn't *discuss,* the Bottleman, the Old-Woman-Dressed-in-Suit-and-Pearls, and the Schoolboy. They didn't *critique.* No. They listened. They laughed. They hooted sometimes. They frowned, when Odysseus was being particularly snotty, obnoxious and deceitful. They sat on the porch, in the *very* late summer sun and they closed their eyes—blind to the street, blind to the city—and they watched the Hero work his wiles. Wine-dark seas ran in their eyelids. (Wine-dampened lips of the Bottleman followed along, whispering the words after Vivian, an echo, as he sipped from his bottle of red.)

And so it went, for nearly a month. The days stayed warm; the crickets filled the night with song. People came. Some of them had money—enough, a few. (Vivian had a bank account; and, she'd been placed on paid sick leave by the University, kind tolerant University. She could survive, a long time, really, on what she had. Flour is cheap; yeast, too—you can even grow it yourself, if you remember to save out some starter dough, every single time you bake.) They read, they ate, they listened. Amanda tapped her way over, bringing her book, and they all listened to "The Dead." Gesundheit curled up under the Schoolboy's feet and the boy's fingers ruffled his soft fur.

These were some of the happiest days of Vivian's life and so of course, they were not to last, were they? Oh, come on, what do *you* think? You know the way the story goes—all this happiness is cloying and slow and, thankfully, short-lived. Because it really is short-lived, isn't it, in life as well? Short-lived, long-loved happiness. Oh well.

Enter the Wolf. You knew he was on his way.

But, oh, not yet. Let's let poor Vivian be happy for just a while longer. Better—let's let her be really, really, really happy. Isn't that what you want, really? Shall we let Vivian fall in love, first, before things get dicey? Can't the woman at least get laid? Yes. All right—put the Wolf on hold.

Enter, instead, the Prince.

Prince Charming

So here he is—a baldish, plumpish lawyer whose wife has just thrown him out of their four-bedroom neocolonial in Clifton Park. Why? Because he quit his job—just walked out one morning, at 11:24, right in the middle of a meeting with the partners in the firm. Yes, the Prince listened carefully to the offer to join the Partners—Barnaby, Dempster, and Bly—and he nodded, calculating the increase in his income and how the news would bring a wide smile to the perfectly painted lips of his wife. Then just as *his* lips—slightly dry, somewhat chapped—were forming the word "Yes," just as "Thank You" and "I'm Honored" were gathering in his throat, the Prince had a vision. He looked out the window into the trees, just beginning to show a hint of autumn color, just beginning to pull in their sap for winter storage, and he saw an image in the glass. He leaned forward, forgetting to nod humbly at Bly, the senior partner.

The image might have been only the reflection of his own face, somehow caught and distorted by the play of fluorescent lights against the September sunshine—but, no, it was not. It was the face of—well, he couldn't say exactly. If he'd been a Hallmark sort of man, he'd have said it was the face of an Angel—all shiny, tingling with light. But very round—and oddly buoyant, as if floating on a long string. A ballooning face, smiling, cheeks puffed out like rich round cheeses. But the Prince was not a man of sentiment. (And if he had been, ten years at the firm of Barnaby, Dempster, and Bly would have put an end to that, wouldn't it?) So, no, the Prince had no name for the face he saw in that smudgy, light-filled pane. But he heard it call to him, in a high, cricketing voice: *Love me, choose me,* it said. *Be my mate.*

Well, you can imagine. Long story short: on that magical morning—did we say that it was the morning of September 20, 2000? Well, it was—the Prince marched out of the firm, tendering his resignation to the secretary on the way out, and informed his wife that he was no longer the income machine she'd come to love. She threw him out, of course, and got lawyers of her own. He landed, about a month later, as outcasts often do, on Sea Street, where the big old houses are, to this day, full of rabbit-hole apartments packed chockablock with people like him—transients, exiles, expatriates, ex-breadwinners, ex-husbands, extras. He landed, in fact, in the street's worst flophouse, located just on the other side of the house full of students where Amanda lived and played her music. Ah, you see. Two doors down from Vivian Worth. Just so.

In his first long lonely nights on Sea Street, as summer finally died and frost moved in, the Prince listened to Amanda's songs. In the early mornings, he awoke to the smell of bread baking. He stretched, as much as he could in a narrow cot in a room so small he could touch a wall with a right hand and another with a left. He stopped being sad, without even trying; his chest, so often tight and crushed in Clifton Park—ribs straining, as if sat upon, always, by the Night Mare herself—that chest expanded in the Sea Street air. He recalled how to breathe. Then, one day, on the morning of October 17, 2000, to be exact, the Prince awoke hungry and happy. He took to the street. Leaves were drifting from the old, old trees, swirling through the air like descending balloons. The air was full of movement, sound. He felt a pull, a kind of tidal force, drawing him along. He went with the tide, easily, like the unfettered bit of flotsam he'd become.

He landed on Viv's porch, of course. He sat on the bottom step, chewing on cinnamon-raisin bread and he listened. Vivian and the Bottleman and Geshundheit were alone this morning. (The Schoolboy had been reprimanded for skipping classes and was back in school. No one had seen the Old-Woman-Dressed-in-Suit-and-Pearls for a while. Well, what of it? People come and go on Sea Street. No one stops them.) The Prince was a bit shy so he didn't climb the steps, but he listened. And he looked at Vivian's face as she read. She was wearing a warm red sweater and her cheeks were pinked by the wind. Her hair kept escaping from its long braid, sailing out in little wisps. She tucked the wisps behind her ears, intent on her book. She was reading about the Sirens. Odysseus tied to the mast, while the Sirens sang their heartbreaking songs. The Prince found himself trembling, found himself falling under the spell of the Sirens' song. Found his penis rising. (Well, no wonder—he hadn't made love to his wife in something like three years. She had smelt like expensive, heavy perfume and her hair was bleached an odd beige color. She worked out incessantly, kept her body so lean and so firm that he couldn't find a handhold, couldn't nestle, couldn't make a dent, really. And he knew that he was just a john, that she only allowed him to fuck her because he paid for it. Paycheck = sex. Simple equation. Understandable but hardly exciting.)

So, here you have it, the moment we've been waiting for, all our lives: Vivian looks down her porch steps at the Prince. He is looking up at her. He is trembling. Their eyes meet and lock. She lowers her voice a touch, letting it get all throaty and sexy. She reads about the Sirens and the man tied to a mast, helpless against their spell. The man on the bottom step—she's noticed him around: a kind-looking, rumpled, dazed sort of man—has a hard-on the size of Calypso's island. She can see it from here.

She leans forward, reading just to him, the ancient Siren-song: *"Pleased by each purling note/ Like Honey twining/ From her throat and my throat,/ Who lies a-pining?"*

The Prince closes his eyes and sighs, from the bottom of his soul.

The Bottleman, who is not stupid, grabs Gesundheit's collar and says, "Guess that's it for me today, Doctor Viv. Off we go." And he leaves. (Good man, good dog.)

And Viv holds out a hand and takes the Prince into her house, up her old wooden stairs and into her bedroom. It is a sunny warm room. The house smells like yeast and flour. When the Prince puts his lips to Vivian's neck, he tastes butter and cinnamon. Her hair is a wild nest of curl, undyed, uncombed. Her skin is like honey, her belly like kneaded dough. He sinks into her, crying out with joy.

So, let's leave them there, shall we? For a while. In perfect, perfect harmony. Fucking like bunnies and reading books.

But you know what's next. We can't hold him off forever. He's coming, with his rank smell and dank fur and fangs. His yellow eyes and hanging lip. His long curling tail—tail like a serpent. Tongue like a snake.

Yes, we can smell him, even over the yeast. He's arrived.

The Wolf

AT FIRST, THERE WEREN'T any wolves in the neighborhood. Well, maybe there were wolf pups. Wolves in training, so to speak. But they weren't particularly ravenous. They were just punks. Teenage boys. One of them, named Robby, lived in the house on the other side of Viv's. (Other meaning the opposite from the house where Amanda lived and played her music.) Robby didn't go to school much. No, Robby and two of his punky friends hung out in the old wooden shed behind Robby's house, where their comings and goings were perfectly visible to Vivian, from her kitchen window. Now that she was home in the mornings, humming happily and kneading dough at the table near the window, she saw Robby and the other punks daily. Did they think that they were invisible, that they'd escaped the eyes of all adults, all authorities, all the grown-ups who thought that boys should go to school? No! They weren't stupid boys, only willfully and stubbornly ignorant. No, they knew that Vivian could see them. And they could see that she didn't care. They could see that she was harmless, a crazy woman who read to the neighborhood nutsos on her porch. A weirdo. Hell, she waved from her window, smiling at them. They kept their dope in the shed; they smoked it without worry, letting its fragrance fill the autumn air, drifting over the backyards, as once the smell of burning leaves had done, when backyard leaf fires were still allowed. Once, even, Robby came to Vivian's door and asked if she had any lighter fluid. They wanted to cook hot dogs, Robby said, on the grill in the shed. But they couldn't get the coals to catch. Vivian had said, sure, sure she had lighter fluid and she'd handed it over. Why not? Vivian was happy these days. She was well-fucked and well-fed and free. She wanted everyone to be the same and she didn't care if boys went to school or not. She thought they were good enough boys. Sly, a little stupid, but not bad. Surely not.

And, truly, they didn't start out as wolves. But there were all those long days in a shed, nothing to do. Boredom. The beginnings of cold weather, as late October brought down the leaves and scattered them on cold morning breath. Where would these pup-punks go, when the shed dripped with icicles? Where would they harbor then? Would they have to give in? Go to school, for the sake of radiators? Find a cave, grow fur?

Well, almost. Because on the morning of November 8—a Wednesday, the day the Prince had gone to court, to be taken, he'd said happily, for everything he owned—Vivian looked out her window and saw that the boys had found a leader. She raised her eyes from the lovely brown dough—whole wheat today—on the bread board, and saw a new boy in the yard. An older boy, lean as a rail. His hair slicked behind his ears. A boy who walked with a limp, hunched against the cold. A boy whose cheeks were gray with stubble. Vivian felt a chill run up her back. She leaned toward the window, her face close to the cold pane.

The older boy—we might as well just call him the Wolf, since you've already guessed who he is—had disappeared into the shed. Robby was leading a chubby little girl across the yard, drawing her slowly toward the shed. The girl was giggling, knee deep in leaves. The wind lifted leaves from the ground and pulled the last remnants from the branches of the old maple that stood in Vivian's yard, but reached its limbs into yards on either side of her own, no regard for fences. The girl's frizzy red hair caught the yellow leaves in its curls—she was crowned with gold-leaf stars, shod in gold-leaf slippers.

Vivian leaned closer to the glass, watching. Her breath misted the pane and she saw through a cloud—the girl might have been eleven, twelve. Maybe less. She was pale, her cheeks dusted with dark freckles. She was fat. She was not pretty, not in any way. But—that crown of stars. No, she was not pretty. But she was beautiful, because she was young. Because she was innocent. A maiden. A virgin. Maybe.

Robby kept a hand on her shoulder. Another boy kept a hand on her elbow. The third had a hand on her back. The three boys all leaned toward the shed, urging the fat girl forward. She hesitated, standing deep in leaves, shaking her head.

Vivian scrubbed her hand over the glass, wiping back the mist. The fat little girl was shaking her head: No. She was planting her feet. No.

But the boys were strong. And persuasive. Robby bent and whispered in the girl's ear. And she giggled. And started to walk again, toward the shed.

No, Vivian thought. No.

But Vivian didn't move fast enough. She'd forgotten how to hurry. She'd relaxed, in her kitchen, on her porch, in her life. Her limbs were often soft, weak with post-sex languor. She moved gently, slowly. She'd forgotten how quickly evil moves, flying like an arrow toward its end.

So she finished kneading the dough. She did a good job, making it smooth and elastic. A breathing living thing. Yeast beasties growing, rising, leavening, lightening. Alive and breathing, set in its warm bowl. Alive, for now, until the fire in the oven would stop it short.

She covered the bowl, tenderly. Set it on the radiator, gently. She washed her hands. She patted back her floury hair.

And only then did she open the back door and step into the wind, heading for the shed. Only then did she act like an adult, like an authority, going to check on the children next door. Only then.

Too late.

Fate

THE FAT GIRL WAS STANDING in the gloom of the shed, a tiny stream of blood running down her thigh. She was staring down at her doughy legs, as if in utter surprise. Her shirt was rucked up about her neck and her little round nipples were bumpy with cold. Her skirt—sad, dusty blue—was rolled to her waist and she was naked below it. She looked up at Vivian, frozen aghast in the doorway of the shed.

Behind the girl, three boys leaned against the wall of the shed, their jeans around their ankles, their pup-pricks in their hands. Next to the girl stood the Wolf. He held a dirty rag. He was wiping blood from his hands and from his long, dangling penis. He had a cigarette in his lips. When he saw Vivian in the doorway, he smiled, a grin like a blade. "You want some too, lady? Or maybe you want to lick me clean?"

The shed was dark. Vivian couldn't be sure, not absolutely certain, of what she saw. In one second, the Wolf had zipped his pants and shoved the rag in his pocket. He'd put a hand on the fat girl's shoulder and shoved. "Get out of here," he said. "You got what you came for. So stop your sniveling and get out."

The girl rolled down her skirt and walked to where Vivian stood. She leaned her head against Vivian's arm, shaking.

Vivian found her voice. "Are you all right?" she said. She put an arm around the child.

The Wolf laughed. "Can't talk, can she? Little cunt's a mute. Right, boys?"

Vivian looked at the three boys. They, too, had tucked their pricks away. They looked like nothing more than boys, scared. Three pale round faces in the gloom of the shed, struck dumb. Cheeses without dial tones. Finally, Robby spoke, voice high and anxious, a terrible whine. "Yeah. That's right. She can't talk. But everybody knows she's a slut. She don't even have a home. She does it with anything that moves. She does it for food. He didn't do nothing more than anyone else does." Robby licked his lips. "And we didn't touch her, I swear." He waved a hand toward his buddies and two other cheese-faces nodded.

Vivian pulled the child against her, backing out of the shed.

Suddenly, the Wolf sprang. He sunk his sharp claws into Vivian's shoulder and breathed his stinking breath into her face. Carrion, meat-rot breath. Poisonous. "You say a word, lady, one fucking word. You make trouble. Just try, okay? I'd love to do you, too. Love it." The gray cheeks pulled in, the fangs gleamed.

Vivian backed all the way to her house, the child with her. She backed into her kitchen and slammed the door.

The girl sat down on a kitchen chair, then smiled, a heart-piercing grin. Blackened teeth. Her eyes, up close, empty and pale. Pink-rimmed. Rabbit eyes.

Vivian leaned forward, brushing a last leaf from the child's hair. "What's your name?" she asked.

The child leaned over the table, put one dirty finger in the flour. She wrote, slowly and deliberately, shaky big letters sketched in the floury surface: *FAY.*

Vivian put the child in the tub, scrubbed her back, soaped her legs. Then she wrapped her in a flannel gown and sent her to sleep in the spare room.

Then she sat down and thought. She could, of course, wait for the Prince to come back and let him do it. She should, of course, let him be the Hero. But, deep in her heart, Vivian knew that he was not the stuff of Heroes. Oh, he was a lovely lover and a wonderful friend and she was crazy about him, but. . . . Well, there's no getting around it, sometimes. The Prince was not a Hero.

She would, she decided, have to take care of this herself.

Oh, you see it, don't you? The terrible mistake? The hubris?

No one. No one should go it alone. No one, intent on Vengeance, should be so foolish. But we are, aren't we? We so often are.

Alone, Vivian shaped her loaves. She let them rise, in their own good time, while she made a plan. Then she slid them into the hot oven. Luckily, the days were very short now and it would be dark by five on Sea Street. Dark before the child named Fay awoke, before the Prince came home.

Vivian had another can of lighter fluid in her basement.

Into the Dark

L OAVES BAKED, WARM AND FRAGRANT on the counter. Child still asleep upstairs.

No signs of Wolf or pups from the shed, all afternoon. They were gone, then. For now. She knew they'd be back. Maybe not the Wolf himself—he'd no doubt moved on, slipping through the dark November afternoon like mist, a miasma of evil. And the pups, scared silly, had scattered. Good enough. She couldn't rid the world of Wolves—even Vivian in all her hubris knew that. But she could get rid of their cave, couldn't she? She could rid the world of just one of evil's hiding places.

Dusk. (It never gets quite dark on Sea Street—the crime lights burn orange all night. But it gets dusky. In dreary November, very dusky. In the backyards, plenty dark enough for a woman with a can of lighter fluid and a pile of rags and a box of matches to slip up to an old wooden shed, unseen.)

Wait: the door to the shed is ajar, moving in the wind, screaking on its rusty hinge. Quickly then: close the door and slide its iron bolt, fast into its slot. There, done, quiet as mouse. The shed is closed up tight. Nothing moves, now, but the woman in the dusk.

It's simple, now—move fast around the outside of the shed. Pile some rags at each corner of the shed, rags in heaps on the cold cold ground. Go in a circle, crouching; cover the compass points, learned as a child. South, north, west, east—everywhere the wind blows. Hold the can of fluid and squeeze. Squirt. Squirt. Squirt. Squirt.

Scrape the matches along the flinty line. Scrape, flare. Scrape, flare. Scrape, flare. Scrape, flare. Step back. Watch. Orange licks appear at each corner. The licks reach up, sniffing the night air. Then they breathe deep—sweet Sea Street air—and they grow, fast.

Smell it!! Fire in the night—leaping up.

Watch. It is pretty. It is. You know it is.

Smile. Dash back to the kitchen. Watch, safe and happy, from behind the pane of glass. Safe inside: friendly old kitchen.

But. . . .

There are screams. Muffled, on the far side of Viv's window glass. Muffled screams, inside the shed with bolted door. Not loud, no. But, still, she can hear them. Screams.

Vivian flings open her back door and the screams are louder. Vivian steps out, onto the frozen grass that crackles beneath her feet.

There are three voices there, inside the shed—high-pitched, terrified pup voices, howling into the night. Rising up with the smoke and the flames, filling the sky. Screaming. Screaming. Screaming.

Vivian would run to save them, really she would. She would, she would—they are only boys. She did not mean this. They are only boys.

But Vivian cannot run. Her arms are held in iron grip.

Fay holds her. She has dug her bare feet into the earth and she is holding Vivian fast. She is grinning. The mute girl is laughing. And she is very strong.

So Vivian cannot run. But she can yell. And that is what she does. She screams into the Sea Street night: *Help them. Help them. Oh please. Help them.*

Heroes: Blind, Beat and Bottled

WELL, SHOULD THEY PERISH for their sins, those silly boys? In the oldest of the tales, they might just. Just might. Small sins, big—in the old tales, Vengeance doesn't pay much attention to the size.

But, it is November 8, 2000—we've grown civilized and soft. We do not think those boys—lost boys, silly boys, stupid boys—quite deserve to be roasted alive, do we? No. No.

But who, who can save them? Vivian cannot, because she is trapped by Fay and her own foolishness. The Prince cannot, because he is not the stuff of Heroes and, besides, he's stuck in divorce court. You cannot, because you are not inside this story—you would if you could, we know that. But you cannot save anyone, can you?

But, wait, someone is coming. Just in time!

Enter the Heroes. There are, in this case, three.

One. The person who pushes a shopping cart, up and down the street. The Bottleman—he can ram his cart into the door of the flaming shed and break the bolt. And he does. But he cannot see the boys inside—they have fallen terribly silent and he cannot find them. The brave Bottleman has done what he can, but he cannot save the boys.

So, two. Who is the one person who can find her way in the dark, led only by her ears and nose and swift booted feet? Led by her magical cane. Amanda, of course. In the dark, the Blind can see. In the fiery, flame-addled dark, the Blind can reach out her fearless cane and reach human flesh. And she can pull the limp bodies out, quickly quickly. One. Two. Three. There—she's got them all. Three boys lie on the grass—and they are all still breathing.

So, why do we need the third Hero?

Ah. Because there is someone else in the shed, still. He hadn't left, after all, the Wolf. He is still in there and he is howling. He, too, is afraid. He, too, reaches a scorching paw and howls for Amanda to pull him out.

And she will, for she is young and brave and Blind and she has never yet met a Wolf. She goes back into the shed and she yells to him: "Grab my hand."

But when he does, he pulls her toward him.

Oh Wolf. You do not want to live, so much as you want to

hurt. Oh, bad bad Wolf.

And Amanda is drawn into the flame and the smoke and her face is crushed up against the Wolf's bony chest and he holds her in his iron arms and he laughs. She chokes, spitting fur and soot and horror. But she cannot escape.

So, the third Hero. This is not a person. It is not an Angel, either, although it looks like one. It is something else although, forever after, no one can agree on what. It seems, from where Vivian stands held in the grip of Fay, to be a balloon. A round thing, made of light. It floats down from the sky. It lands on the shed, a perfect circle of white in the orange flame.

It—this is very hard to describe, so you must use your imaginations—whooshes, a great release of air, a sudden whirlwind of gases. And it sucks the flames away from the shed. The flames do not die out—no, they lift. They sail away, up and up and up into the night sky. They flash like the tail of a comet and they disappear. The ashes of the shed steam gently in the cold night air.

Amanda staggers out into the arms of the Bottleman, coughing, alive. She shakes her head. "What the fuck was *that*?" she says.

And all of them—even the three boys, who have awakened in time to see the ball of light explode into the sky—shake their heads. No one knows what the fuck that was.

Some kind of balloon, they all agree, later. Some kind of helium-hearted miracle.

Happily Ever After, Again

So. This is how it all turns out. You already know that Amanda's band makes it big. Good for her. She deserves it. She still practices, six hours a day. She is a pro.

The three boys? They are all scarred. Not badly, but enough. Each bears on his face a star-shaped patch of burned skin. Their scars pull and tighten, throbbing. They will ache, always. They remind. Every day of their lives, they remind. They remain.

The Bottleman, oddly enough, ends up marrying the Beatwoman. (A story for another time, perhaps?) Gesundheit has an unexpected litter of pups. Good dog.

The Schoolboy and his family adopt Fay. The Schoolboy teaches her to speak, by reading to her, day and night. He loves her dearly, and she him. The very first words she ever speaks are his true name, which even we do not know.

Vivian, of course, lives with her Prince, although they decide never to marry. They are too smart to fall for that old trick. But they cannot live on love alone. They open a law office/library/bakery combo, right here on Sea Street. Good—they can live on what they take in, little as it is.

But they don't have to, for long. For Vivian inherits a great fortune: the Old-Woman-in-Suit-and-Pearls—remember?—was lying dead in her bed, those days when no one saw her. She'd died gently, in her sleep. And, yes, she'd made a will, on one of those late October nights when the crickets were still singing. She really did love those stories she heard on Vivian's porch. She really did.

And the Wolf? No one knows. No one saw him go, that night in November. But no bones were found in the rubble of the shed, no scorched hide. Still, the Wolf is gone, for now. For now.

The End

I T IS DECEMBER 21, 2000. Late, late at night. The winter solstice. The longest, darkest night of the year. A magical, miracle, marvelous night. Sea Street is asleep and snow is falling.

Vivian stands alone in her backyard. She spreads her arms wide. The snow coats her shoulders, a cold white lacy shawl. She welcomes the coming year.

Leave It Lie

I**T'S SO COLD THAT** the plastic trash bags crack when I pick them up, their edges sharp. So cold the three layers of t-shirt, turtleneck and flannel I wear under my Carhartts don't do much to stop my shivering. See, you never get used to the cold when you hop in and out of the truck on a night like this. Inside, the heater's blasting and Echo's smoking and singing and it's hot; outside, the wind screams down Manning Boulevard, slicing as it comes. The stars are like chips of white ice in a black sky. You're out there grabbing bags as fast as you can with your hands all clumsy in their frozen leather gloves and you see warm yellow lights in the big brick houses and sometimes you want to break in, sneak your smelly, trashman self into their houses and sit in front of their fireplaces, get warm. Then you're back in the truck and your gloves start to drip and stink and then you're back outside. See? Nights like this just keep tipping the balance and you can never get a grip, one way or the other.

This night, February something, a Wednesday—I know that, because Wednesday is trash night in the fancy neighborhoods—Echo's into Bruce Springsteen, singing about how he was born to run. This is pretty damn funny, if you've ever seen Echo: he's over sixty, three hundred pounds, about four teeth in his head and only two of them meet. Just enough to hold a cigarette or a joint. Echo never leaves the cab of the truck. Ever. Once, last fall, I got smacked in the mouth by a branch. I was bleeding all over myself, kind of yelling for him to help, and Echo just leaned over the seat and threw a rag out the window. "You hold that real tight, until you got that mess stopped. Don't get none of your nasty blood in my truck." Anyway, this night, the wind is something fierce and clouds shoot across the sky, aiming for the river, going east. I climb inside the truck and look down the street. It's a long, wide street, hilly, with all these big houses on both sides. And it's got a little divider running down the middle, flowers and grass in summer, rock-solid snow banks now. It's funny how the snow in these people's front yards stays white and clean—no tracks. No one ever messes them up and the front yards glow. The snow banks by the road are black, all crusty from street sand and crud. Everything's either black or white out here in February; in the middle of the night, everything's opposites. Like me and Echo. Fat and skinny. Old and young. A singer and a mute.

Not really. I can speak. I just don't, much.

Anyway, I look down Manning and, swear to God, the weirdest thing happens. Way down the street, where the houses are biggest and brickiest, I see someone running down the sidewalk. It's a blur, but it looks like a woman in a long white nightgown and she's sprinting, garbage bag in hand. She looks all squared off somehow, like a sail in the wind. The whole thing is so weird that I actually say something aloud to Echo: "Hey, man, look at that!"

Echo kind of jumps. *"Baby, we were born to. . . .* What?"

I point, but the woman—if that's what it was—is already gone. I tried to watch her go but her white nightgown just disappeared into the white snow of some front yard. "That woman," I say. I point, up ahead.

Echo leans way forward, grunting his big belly up against the steering wheel. "Don't see nobody," he says.

So we just keep on crawling down the street and I keep on grabbing hold of crackling-cold bags and icy silver cans. But near the end of the street, I know right away when I touch the bag that woman was carrying: it's not even cold yet. It's still flexible. I pick it up and then I feel the jolt in my belly—like a big kick. Because that bag is moving. And squeaking.

I hold it out at arm's length, and look at it. The wind slices at my ears and cheeks and tears start coming from my eyes. The bag is heavy and wet at the bottom, I can tell by that sloshy feeling it has. It hasn't frozen yet.

The window on my side of the truck opens and Echo yells out. "Get your ass in here, boy. What the fuck you doing?"

I hold up the bag, I'm showing it to him, and I say, "There's something alive in this bag, man."

He grunts. "Well, I don't want to know what it is. Might be somebody's pet ferret they got sick of, some kind of nasty thing. Throw it in back."

I put my hands under the bag and, really, it's right then that I know. I feel little feet. I pull the bag to my chest and run my hands under it. Little head. I start to shake, partly maybe from the cold, but mostly because I just do. And I can't talk anymore. And I can't seem to move. I just wrap the bag in my arms.

Next thing I know, Echo is actually out of the truck and he's standing next to me, blocking the wind, pulling on my arm. "Man, you're freaking me out," he says. "Move now, asshole. I can't be standing out here in this shit. It's taking my breath." He tries to take the bag out of my arms, but I hold it tighter. It's still warm in there, inside that black plastic. "All right, then," Echo says, real quiet. "All right. Just bring the bag into the truck, all right? Come on now, man."

And then I'm sitting in the blast from the heater and Echo's climbing back inside, too, all puffing and grunting. The bag moves a little, on my lap. I peel off my stinking gloves and open the bag. There's no trash it in. It's clean, straight from the box. Way down inside, though, there are feet. I reach in and feel around. Everything's kind of damp down there and it smells like salt and blood. And, goddamn if there isn't four feet in there: each one about as big as the top of my thumb. Two feet are warm, two are cold. I pull my hand back out. I turn to Echo. "Babies," I say.

"Holy Mother." Echo grabs the bag right out of my hands and he reaches in. Just one of Echo's hands is big as both of mine and swear to God he brings up two babies at once. In one huge palm, two babies.

I stare at them lying in Echo's big hand. One is a boy baby, all kind of dark blue, and not moving. The other one, the girl, has feet that kick a little and her tiny face is squinched up and she's making some kind of noise.

Echo takes his other hand, real slow, and lifts up the boy baby. "Open your shirt," he says.

"What?"

"Right to skin, man. Right now. Open up."

You got to listen to Echo when he's all calm and serious like this. I unzip my Carhartts, unbutton the flannel, pull up the turtleneck and t-shirt around my neck. My skinny white chest glows green in the truck light. Echo hands me the boy baby first and I take it in my left hand. Then he hands me the girl and I take her in my right. I sit there like an idiot, just holding them.

Echo says, real quiet: "Put them against your skin and hold them."

I cross my arms so the boy ends up on the right and the girl on the left. Then Echo pulls my t-shirt and turtleneck down over me. It feels like I'm dead for a minute, hands crossed on my chest, not able to move. But then the girl baby stirs. I feel her little head turning, against my skin. She's warm. The boy baby feels like a piece of raw chicken straight from the fridge. I get goose bumps all down my right side, from him. But I keep on holding him. Holding them both. For a second, I think of Darla—that's my girlfriend—and how she used to wrap herself around my back in her sleep, both her hands closed into warm fists against my chest, her breath damp between my shoulder blades. I think how she doesn't sleep like that anymore and how maybe that's why my chest feels like it's got holes in it most of the time.

Echo has slammed the truck into gear and we're moving, fast. Not stopping for any more bags. He makes that big old truck move out and before I really have time to think, about anything, we're at the emergency room of Saint Peter's hospital, pulled up at a spot that says "Ambulances Only." Echo actually jumps out of the truck and he rumbles off to get us some help. I watch out of the front window of the truck. It's funny, in the blue light from the ER sign, it's just like looking at a TV. I see Echo's big body barrel through those doors that slide open by themselves and I see about four security guys in dark blue uniforms, they come running and one puts his hands on Echo's chest, holding him back. And I'm afraid that Echo's going to floor the guy right there but then I see that Echo's talking fast and I can see when they actually start to listen and then I see a nurse, pretty, long hair in a braid down her back, start to run toward the truck.

But it's hard to concentrate because inside my shirt, the girl baby has a hold of my nipple and she's sucking. I can't feel anything but that sudden, wet pulling on my chest. She's hanging on for all she's worth. And it's funny. I feel bad, sorry I can't make milk for her, she's trying so hard. And when the pretty-haired nurse swings herself into the truck cab, I feel sorry that I smell like garbage and that I never bother to shower before work.

I GET HOME way later than usual but Darla doesn't even turn over in bed when I slide in next to her. She works four to midnight, cleaning offices at the college up the road. It's five in the morning, not light yet, and she's out. I'm wired as hell and dying to tell her about the twins but I can't wake her, not yet. So I try to just lie there, try to stop shaking. But I keep running my hands over my bare chest. I keep feeling them there, still: warm and cold, on my skin. I keep seeing them in Echo's hands.

I didn't get to see them again, in the ER. They were rushed off somewhere. Then I talked for a long time to two cops and that made me nervous as hell. I mean, I know I didn't do anything wrong. And maybe, like Echo says, we're fucking heroes. But still. Cops. And they'll go off somewhere and look us up, Echo and me, and see that we both have records, both spent a little time away and I just don't think heroes is what we'll end up being. And at first Echo kept saying he never saw no woman and I kept saying I did and so the story sounded kind of fishy, but then Echo started saying, yeah, yeah, maybe he did see that woman, out of the corner of his eye, running along all in white, long black hair all wild down her back, and I know he's making that up because he wants to be part of the reward or whatever and now the story sounds to me like a lie, but the cops like it better this way, because it all matches. After a long time, the pretty nurse comes back, her face sort of sad, and tells me that the boy baby was dead—probably never breathed at all, she says. Not even once. Then she smiles and says that the girl baby is alive and in the neo-something something and they think she'll make it. Says the girl weighs about two and a half pounds and she's breathing on her own. And then that nurse puts her nice clean hand on my dirty arm and says, "You guys did a great job. You saved her." And then the cops kind of shut up and they let us go home.

I roll over and put my face against Darla's shoulder. I'll say this right here: Darla's the best thing that ever happened to me. Ever. She's made my ratty little apartment into a home. She's smart and she's loyal and she works hard. Darla always tells me that she's going somewhere, in life, and she's hoping to take me with her. Well, no. She used to say that. I haven't heard that in a while, how *we're* going somewhere. I think, even while I'm tasting Darla's skin, that *she's* going somewhere, for sure, and soon. As soon as she's got someplace of her own to go. That's what I taste on her shoulder—her going.

My mouth gets dry on her skin and my eyes get wet. Because right now, she just smells so damn good; she always showers after work, sometime after midnight. I didn't, tonight. Didn't want to wash away that baby's spit—her little mouth-pull on my poor old useless dry nipple. I feel like I might sleep, but then I think, all of a sudden, about all the pissed-off Manning Boulevard people who are about to wake up and see that their trash is still on the street. These are just the kinds of people to call Department of Public Works and I think that me and Echo are going to get canned. But then I think that maybe we won't, heroes that we are and all. And then I can't help it and I kind of nudge Darla hard and she groans and pushes her hair out of her face. "Hi," she says. She turns around to face me and snuggles her face into my chest and I kind of freeze because her nose is right about where that cold dead baby was and I think she'd hate that.

See, here's the thing. I'm not supposed to know that Darla had an abortion last month. But I do know because I heard her snuffling into the phone to her sister in Jersey, telling her that she had to, she just had to, there was no way it could work. I heard her say she wasn't ready, it was a big mistake and she couldn't keep it—she just could not do it. But she never told me and so I keep my mouth shut. But she's been prickly ever since. And, swear to God, she's started mooning around the church behind our apartment. We live on Dove, in a basement apartment. Behind us, there's this big old Catholic church with a great big stained glass window. When they've got the lights on in the church, like they do sometimes at night—I don't know why, weddings maybe—we can see the picture from that window. It glows real bright and our whole little scroungy backyard and dark little kitchen turn all kinds of colors. Anyway, me and Darla love the window and all, but I never thought to see her sniffing around the front door of the church. And I guess it's got to do with the abortion that, officially, I don't know about. And that started her leaving me, bit by bit.

And maybe it's bad that my girlfriend lied to me about something that big. I mean, it was my baby, too, right? And, yes, it's a lie not to tell someone something like that. You don't have to speak a lie to be untrue, everybody knows that. But I can't hold myself up as the non-liar in the house. I never told Darla exactly what happened when I was at Brookwood. That's the so-called farm where they send kids, instead of jail. I mean, she knows I went there and she knows why: me and couple of my buddies got high when we were sixteen and broke into a house. We didn't get much, even. Except sent to the farm. She knows I'm a garbage man because it's hard for me to get any other job—no high school diploma. She thinks it was just kid stuff, all that history—and it was. And I'm over eighteen now, so it's in the past. She has a little bit of a past, too, and that's why she's cleaning offices at the college instead of sitting in one of the classrooms, with other smart girls her age. But what I don't tell her about is some of the shit that happened at the farm. To me. And to other kids. Like this: I saw a kid die there. I was in the room. I didn't do it, but I didn't stop it either. There was a bunch of guys, kicking, and two or three, holding him down. He'd been ratting on kids, I heard. He'd brownnosed up to the counselors and turned on the boys. It didn't have anything to do with me, not really. But I still see the surprised look on that kid's face, like he just couldn't believe he was dying, at fifteen.

I shift a little, so that Darla's face is up near my neck and away from the cold baby spot and then I fall asleep. Light's just creeping into the sky when I drift away. And the wind's still howling.

DOORBELL RINGS AT something like 8:30 a.m. Darla didn't use to get up until noon, but lately, she's always up early. She's got books in the kitchen and she's reading them, mornings. So she's awake and dressed and everything and she goes up the stairs to the front door and then she comes back down to the bedroom and shakes my shoulder.

"Jesus, Gary," she says. "There's a reporter from the *Times-Union* here. He says you're a hero. What the hell happened?"

I sit up and it all comes back: how cold and windy and black the night was. I shake my head. Darla pushes her hair away from her face—it's brown and curly. Her hair softens up her face, which, I have to be honest here, is pretty sharp and beaky otherwise. She just got glasses, last week, and she keeps pushing them up her nose.

"What happened?"

I put a hand under her chin and smooth her face. "We found two babies," I say. "In a trash bag. Me and Echo."

Her whole head goes still and I can see her eyes behind her glasses freeze in their sockets. "Where?" she says.

"On Manning. Right on the street. Twins."

Something relaxes in her face and I feel so bad I could just fucking cry because I know what she was thinking, just for that one second when she froze: she was thinking that I collected the trash outside some place where they do abortions. She knows my route and she knows that can't be what happened but I know that's what she thought, for one terrible second, when I said "baby" and "trash bag" in the same sentence. I can't even think about it, it scares me so much, how she looked. So I talk faster. "And we took them to Saint Peter's and one's going to live, they think. A little girl."

She stands up and I can see her thin shoulders pull back. She's straightening up, tugging herself into shape. "Wow," she says. "You better come talk to this guy. I've got coffee made."

I don't want to brag but the guy kind of leads me into it. He tells me what Echo said—and Echo's remembering more and more about last night, like how he pointed out the moving bag and how he knew all along that it had babies in it. I can feel Darla listening. She's leaning on the kitchen counter and me and the reporter are at the big cardboard box we call a table—Darla puts tablecloths on it and all—but she's listening. She's so still I can feel her breathing back there, can kind of hear her ribs creaking in and out. I just tell him what I remember. But I don't contradict Echo because, hell, he has a right to his own story, doesn't he? And just before the reporter leaves, when I've walked him out to our icy little doorway, I ask him how the baby's doing and he says she's holding on. And then he tells me that the nurses named her Valentine, for now. Because today's Valentine's Day, and it's a good thing he reminded me so I can get Darla something. He asks if they can send a photographer to take my picture later. I say no thanks.

I walk with him to the sidewalk in front. The air is warmer today. The wind's dying down. He says there will be a story in tomorrow's paper. "Stay tuned," he says. "See you in the funny papers."

When I get back to the kitchen, Darla's not there anymore. She's in the shower. I can hear the water running. And that's funny, because she never bothers to shower before work. But today she is and I stand outside the door and listen to the water and smell her shampoo on the steam that leaks out the crack around the door. And, when she comes out, her eyes all red, I don't know what to say. So I keep my mouth shut. And she spends the rest of the morning reading those books—the ones she takes from one of the professors' offices at the college. She takes a few every week; she brings them home and reads them and then she takes them back. It's not stealing, she says. It's like a library. Those professors, she says, they have so many books they lose count.

This week, it's mythology books. I don't know exactly what that means. Then she says a funny thing: she says that in these myths, these stories she's reading, that twins are always sort of magical, sort of fated to do great things. She rests her sharp little chin in her hand and she pushes her new glasses up her long nose and she says, "Or, terrible things."

I want to keep in the conversation and so I say, "Like what? What kinds of things?"

She smiles. "They get raised by wolves. They found cities." Then she frowns. "If they're boys. If they're girls, I don't know. Sometimes, they get turned into stars. Constellations."

"Holy shit," I say. It isn't the brightest remark, I know, but I'm having a hard time keeping up here. To tell the truth, this happens a lot lately: Darla's reading all these books and she's all the time talking about things I don't get.

She kind of smiles again and it's not the nicest smile. It's kind of superior coyote-smile. Like she knows I don't know shit and kind of likes that I don't. What Darla doesn't get is that I'm *proud* that she knows this kind of shit. Not mad, not embarrassed: proud. "Right," she says. "Holy shit." She looks down at her book again. She says the next word all slow: "Metamorphoses."

"Huh," I say. I'm not even going to try with that one. But she's wrong if she thinks I totally don't get it. I do: I can see those twin babies floating up to the sky, some day. Both of them smiling. Twinkle twinkle, little stars. I shake my head. I'm tired.

It's a weird surprise when my boss calls and says the department is giving me and Echo a nice bonus. Because, he says, we deserve it, for all the good publicity we're bringing to the department. He's cheerful as shit and I hardly recognize his voice.

I'm TIRED BUT I can't nap and I've got most of the day before I head back to work, so I take a long hot shower and I put on the clothes that Darla's brought back from the laundromat, all clean and pressed. Darla likes to iron, believe it or not. She always stands there ironing, her eyes focused on something I can't see, humming. She makes the kitchen smell like clean, hot cotton. Like a real home somehow. Anyway, when I'm decent, I take the bus to Saint Peter's and I ask the woman at the front desk about the baby girl and when I tell her who I am, she smiles and pats my arm and tells me, follow the signs that say NEONATAL INTENSIVE CARE UNIT. She even tells me that she'll call up there in advance so they'll let me in. Just like you were the daddy, she says. And her smile makes my eyes sting.

The nurses make a fuss about me. They put a yellow gown over my clean clothes and they tie the little strings in back and then they walk me over to a glass box. They've hung a whole lot of red and pink hearts over the box, cheery and cute. I'm still scared to see her, little Valentine. But I look anyway. She's got a needle in her head, sticking right into one of the tiniest little blue veins you ever saw. And wires and machines everywhere, lit up and beeping. And a little mask over her eyes. I hate that mask—that just seems wrong. All I can really see that looks like a normal baby is her two pink feet and a little bit of fuzzy brown hair on the back of her head. One nurse, an older woman in a shirt with pink and blue bunnies all over it, leans over the box and kind of clucks at the baby. "She's doing just fine," she says. "She's a strong girl."

"Why are her eyes covered?" I'm thinking that maybe Valentine went blind, somehow. That the inside of that black bag just killed her eyes or something, it was so dark and so cold.

The nurse smiles. "Oh, the lights are so bright in here and when you give babies oxygen, it can hurt their eyes. It's just a precaution."

"She's not blind?"

"Lord, no, honey. This little girl is just fine."

Just then there's a big fuss at the door and the nurse walks away. I finally look around and notice three other babies in glass boxes. No one else has pink and red hearts, though, and I feel kind of proud, like my baby is special. Then there's Echo and it's the funniest thing I ever saw and I actually laugh out loud. Echo is wearing a yellow gown, too—but it doesn't half fit him and it's flapping around in front like a yellow apron, strings all loose, and he's grinning ear to ear. I don't think such a big man was ever in this place before. Looks like if he takes a step, all the little glass boxes will topple and fall over, babies and all. But that bunny-shirt nurse, smiling and kind of flirty, she takes Echo by the hand and leads him between the boxes. And that's what makes me laugh—Echo has to tiptoe along, holding his arms tight against his belly. He looks like a yellow-bellied elephant and it's comical as hell.

He comes up and pops me on the arm, a solid punch. "Hey, man," he says. Then he leans right down over Valentine's box and he says, "Ah, man, she's cute."

Now this is a pure lie. That baby isn't cute, not in the state they've got her in. But that's what Echo says. And then he pulls my arm and says, "Come on out in the hall. They're waiting."

So I follow him out, watching his wide ass skim those glass boxes all the way. In the hall, there's the reporter I talked to this morning and a guy with a whole bunch of cameras. Echo grabs me and puts his heavy arm on my shoulders and the guy takes a whole lot of shots, fast. My eyes blink with every one and I wish they'd given me one of those eye masks, too, because I feel like I might go blind, right here in the hallway.

Echo asks the reporter something I never would have: "Hey, they found out who's this baby's mama?"

The reporter shakes his head. "Nope. The police are going door-to-door on Manning, asking questions. But I haven't heard that they found her yet."

Funny, I'd almost forgot that Valentine had a mama. More like she—and her little brother—just dropped out of the sky. But there was that lady, running in the dark in her white nightgown. I hope they never find her. Hell, she's had enough trouble already. Let it go, man, I want to say. Leave it lie. But the words don't come out.

"Huh." Echo runs a hand down his little yellow gown. "So what'll happen to her?"

The reporter shrugs. "Foster care, I guess. Then some family will adopt her." He grins. "She'll be in the paper; she's cute. Some rich family with no kids will take her."

"And she'll grow up all pampered. Nice." Echo's pulling his gown off his shoulders.

"Yes, yes it is. Well, thank you, gentlemen. See you in the funny papers." The reporter nods to the camera guy and they both walk off down the hall.

"Asshole," Echo says. "He loves to say that line, you can tell." He's got the gown off and he shoves it into a bin outside the door of the room where the babies are. "Want to get a beer?" he says to me.

I can hardly think what to say. Echo's never asked me to go

anywhere or do anything. "No, thanks," I say.

He shrugs and goes off down the hall. I watch his back: it's like a huge boulder rolling away down the shining bright hall. I reach behind me and struggle with the gown's strings. They're all in knots and I have to break one to get the thing off. And then the thin yellow cotton tears. I take the ruined gown and push it way down into the bin, under the others. I do that at home, too, always have. I hide things I break. Darla noticed, once, when I shoved a cracked plate under the coffee grounds in our trash. Her eyes got all sorry and she said, "Things break, Gary. And it's not always your fault."

But sometimes it is, my fault. I know that I should just go, leave this hospital before I really mess up. But I can't help it. I lean just a little bit into the baby room and say, "Excuse me?"

The bunny nurse looks up. "Yes, sweetheart?" she says.

These words are the hardest I've had to say but I get them out. "Do they ever let the person who found the baby adopt the baby?"

Her whole face goes sad and she comes right over to the door. "Oh, honey," she says. "You're single, right? You're, what, twenty years old?"

"Nineteen."

She touches my shoulder. "Listen. That baby girl will go to the best family in the world. She'll grow up clean and smart. She'll go to college and she'll have a fine life. Don't you worry about her."

I nod. But I'm not really worrying about her. That's the thing. I'm worrying about me. And Darla. Because just for a minute, I wanted to take this baby home. Our Valentine.

WHAT I DO, instead, is get a bunch of pink flowers and a big red heart-shaped balloon at the hospital gift shop. Darla's already at work when I get home and I put the flowers in a glass and put them on the table. I tie the ribbon that's hanging from the balloon to the back of a chair. It floats around up there, bright and shiny, but when it turns I see that it says GET WELL SOON on one side. So I have to take it down. I don't know exactly how to get rid of it then. It's so big and bouncy. I let it float around up by the ceiling for a while.

Darla calls on her break. Her voice is all excited. She starts talking the minute I pick up the phone, something about the religious studies building and some new books she found, on and on about what she's reading. I lose track, but I keep saying, "Hey, that's great, baby" and "Uh huh" every few minutes, just so she'll remember I'm there.

After she hangs up, I take the balloon outside. I stand on the little scrap of cement we call our backyard. Funny, it's getting much warmer out here. That nasty-ass wind's gone and the air is sort of soft, damp. Water's dripping off the roof and running down the gray stone walls of the church. That's what it's like around here: winter comes and goes. Keeping you off balance. I'm holding on to the ribbon that hangs from the balloon, but it wants to get away. It's lifting for the sky, a heart-shaped sail. I'm thinking that maybe if Darla thinks I'm a hero, just a little bit, she'll hang around. Maybe just out of curiosity, to see how it all turns out. I almost laugh, it's so perfect when I let the balloon go and it lifts up, flying over the church roof and into the sky. Get well soon. Who says I'm too dumb for symbolism?

WHEN DARLA COMES home, around eight, I've got our little kitchen all fixed nice. There's the flowers and a box of chocolates I got at the drug store to replace the balloon. I got a whole box of Valentines too, the kind you used to give out in elementary school: dinosaurs and monsters and dogs and cats, all saying funny things. On every one, I wrote: GARY LOVES DARLA in big scribbly letters, just like third grade. I scattered them all over the table, around the box of Kentucky Fried I bought. I even found candles and I light them when I hear her key in the lock.

Darla's eyes get all round, under her new glasses. She stops in her tracks. She's holding a big fat bag of books in her arms. "Oh, Gary," she says. "Shit. I forgot what day it is."

I feel it, I won't say I don't. I feel it and it hurts but I just smile. "That's okay, baby. You've had a big day."

She drops the books and comes round the table and puts her arms around me. She smells like soap. Her hair curls into my chest and I hold on.

After the chicken, we go outside. Darla says since it's warmed up so nice, we should get some air. In the church, there must have been a night wedding or something. Makes sense—Valentine's Day. There's still a light on in there and the big round window shines, red and green and blue and yellow on the dripping wet cement of our yard. Darla's face, when she turns it to me, is striped with color. She shines, she really does.

BUT I'VE GOT to go to work. We're supposed to do the downtown route tonight, all around the South End. Poor folks, ratty neighborhood. And Echo's got some kind of bug up his ass, some kind of hero bug. He's been loving this shit. And now he wants more of it. Wants to "solve the fucking case," he says. Says he always wanted to be a detective. So he swings the truck north, heading in the direction of Manning Boulevard. I don't like it, but he's in charge.

At least it's not so cold tonight. And I don't have to get out of the truck. Tom Petty and the Heartbreakers are singing in the cab. When we get to the part of Manning where we picked up little Valentine and her brother, Echo slows the truck to about three miles an hour and starts asking: "Is it that house? That one? That one?"

And, see, I really can't remember. It's like trying to bring back a dream—all the details are wrong. But I don't want to disappoint him. I don't want to disappoint any fucking body, ever again. So, I close my eyes and I try to see her, that woman running with a trash bag in her hand. I try to picture her feet in the snow. I see it again, only this time, I think that I really can see her: she's got long black hair and there are little drops of blood in the snow, everywhere she steps. I can track her, easy.

I open my eyes: the snow is all slushy, now. All that black and white, it's smudged to plain old gray. There won't be a footprint left. It's hopeless. Finally, I point to one of the biggest of the big houses, just ahead on our left, and I say, "Maybe that one?"

And Echo says, "Shit, man." And kind of shrinks down in the seat.

Because what I hadn't seen is there's a police car up in the driveway of that house. Just one car, way up the curving drive. All the lights in the house are on.

Echo backs up and then pulls the truck over to the side of

the street, lights out. Me and him, we don't want to talk to cops, not ever again. So we just sit there in the truck and we watch from about five houses down. And we listen because now there are sirens. And then lights. Three more cop cars. An ambulance.

Echo slides farther down in the seat and sighs. "Oh, yeah. It figures. She went and tried to off herself. Women," he says, shaking his head. "You can't never tell what they're going to do."

I don't know if that's it at all. Don't even know if it's the right house. But I sit quiet and watch. The ambulance guys go into the front door of the house, running. We wait. They come out carrying a stretcher. There's someone on it, covered with a big white sheet.

"Do you think she's dead?" I say.

Echo says, "Nah. See, they didn't have her face covered up."

I don't see how he can see this, this far away, but maybe. Maybe his eyes are just that much better than mine.

In a couple of seconds, the stretcher is tucked into the ambulance and they're off. Straight to Saint Peter's, I guess. I wonder if she'll get to see Valentine. I wonder if, someday, they'll even let her take her baby home.

The cop cars all pull away.

Echo starts the truck. Sighs. "That's that," he says.

"But she's not dead, right?"

He looks at me. "I already told you, man. They didn't cover her face. Just leave it alone. All right?"

I nod. Don't even try to answer.

THE NEXT MORNING, Darla runs out to buy a paper and then she climbs back into bed so we can read it together. It has the story about Valentine and the pictures from the hospital. There's her little glass box, pink and red hearts hanging over it. There's me, tucked under Echo's big arm like he's a tree and I'm a stick. He's grinning. My eyes are closed. We're wearing those stupid yellow gowns.

There isn't anything in the paper about the baby's mother and I'm glad about that, since I haven't said one word to Darla about the cops or the ambulance or any of that. Maybe the reporters just haven't caught up with that part yet. Or maybe all they care about is the baby. A baby makes a better story.

Darla takes one of her fingers and pushes up her glasses, looking at me. "You're a star," she says.

See you in the funny papers, I think. I shake my head. "Not me."

The thing is, she doesn't even bother to argue. "It's the beginning of something, though," she says. "I wish I were the Sybil, you know? So I could prophesy. See the future, know when somebody's in trouble before it gets real bad. I wish that I could do something like that, save somebody. Anybody."

This is my moment, the exact time that I should tell her that she can. She can save somebody. But the words don't form. I just pull her down and hold her. I can feel her breasts on my chest, warm. Except that I can still feel the cold spot, too, the spot where the baby who didn't live, who never even took one breath of air, left its mark.

I can't see the future, myself. Don't want to.

What I want is to say: I'm sorry, baby. I am so sorry.

But I don't. I just leave it lie.

Fatty Lumpkin vs. The Reaper:

Rounds One, Two and Three

Fatty Lumpkin is blind as a biscuit. Looks like one, too, in his old age: puffy with extra weight, once-white fur gone yellow, brown spots like crust around his edges. And so what? He doesn't mind being blind; doesn't know he's fat; loves life as he always did. So what if his old eyes see only fog? So what? Walks still smell the same—nice little notecards of pee are still left for him every day by the other neighborhood dogs and cat-stink footpaths still rim his sidewalks. There will always be rank squirrel trails, calling to be followed. On trash days, lovely bits of garbage still wait to be hoovered into his low-slung maw.

Walks sound the same, too, mostly. Bus brakes squealing at the corners and so on.

Fatty Lumpkin lives a happy life, despite being lardy and blind. He sleeps a great deal, eats even more. He most certainly does not seem like a dog who will have to pull a Lassie, have to rescue his people from death, destruction, whatever. He doesn't have a "Yo Rinny" bone in his body. Nor does he possess the calm countenance of the Seeing Eye. Or the anxious tail-wag of the cave-rescue dog. God knows, not the noble sadness of the cadaver dog sent to disaster zones, nose twitching among corpse-strewn rubble. No K-9 he.

But, still, we don't get to choose, do we? Dog or human, we are most often thrust into trouble, willy-nilly, bing bang boom. Pup or person, we're just tossed right in, feetfirst. Forced to stand or to flee. Hero or goat, nothing in between. Flight, or fight.

When his moment came, Fatty fought. His ancient terrier blood arose; he smelled a rat; he dug in; he set his teeth; he closed his foggy eyes and locked his creaky jaw. He held on.

That none of his people knew what heroism he'd shown, or ever would, didn't matter in the least. People hardly ever know what dogs do.

People are a permanently blind species, after all.

One

It's NOVEMBER 7, a Saturday night, and Gracie is taking her old dog for his evening walk. She moves quickly along the greasy cold sidewalks; it's dark early—here it is only 5:30 or so and full night already—and the streets below Grand Street get dicey after dark. Even in this nasty wind tearing the scarf from her head, there are groups of shadowy men and boys on corners and she hates to walk by those. She could choke, just smelling the bottles they tip to their mouths, just listening to their low-pitched laughs. Their faces lit from below by the flames of their smokes, the orange-blue flash of a match. And, oh Lord, half a block down, there's a car idling; a young woman in a bathrobe dashes out from her apartment-house doorway and leans into the window of the car. A second later, that girl is running back into her building, holding a small something in the pocket of her robe. The car guns away, loud music booming in its wake. The words of the song linger, scratching against Gracie's cold ears as she hurries along: *nigger, bitch, motherfucking this, motherfucking that, motherfucking everything, splat splat splat.* At least that's what it sounds like to her and it creeps inside her head and she knows she'll hear it all night long.

"Come on, Fatty," she says to the dog, yanking his leash. Her nylon-clad ankles are cold and wet, bulging as they do above the furry tops of her boots. Her feet hurt. Her back, neck and jaw hurt. She aches, just about everywhere, out in this cold damp. "We got to get home now. They're waiting on us to get supper on, you know that."

Fatty's nose stays firmly glued to the sidewalk. He's busy smelling the footprints of that young woman in the robe. She'd run out of the house barefoot and her invisible trail is rich with smells. Fatty knows that she had chicken and rice for lunch, spiced up good, from the Jamaican place on the corner, but that it hasn't sat well in her stomach. And he knows that she's been waiting all day for that car to come; he can smell the desperate chill sweat that's been coating the skin of her feet, all this long waiting day.

"Come on." Gracie pulls the leash harder.

Fatty lifts his head and then he sees it: right through the dark fog that coats his eyes, he sees the tall black shape leaning against the telephone pole. No—not leaning really, that's not it. The shape surrounds the pole like a thick curtain. Fatty feels a growl crawling up his throat, unbidden. Then he smells it. The shape stinks. It's a sulfurous rotten-egg, burning-tire chemical stink that shoots up into Fatty's nostrils like acid. And the acid is underlaid with something musty, something moldering.

Then he hears it: the shape makes a sharp hissing noise. The fur on Fatty's neck rises into sharp points. The shape moves; it seems to reach out toward Gracie, one long swirling black arm. Now Fatty's fur is a long line of bristling rage—head to tail. He has grown spines of furious, terrified terrier fur. A growl opens his teeth and emerges into the night air.

Gracie looks down. Her little dog's teeth are bared and he feels like an arrow on the end of his leash. He's staring at a telephone pole and making a strange low noise she's never heard before in her life. She can't see a thing wrong with that pole, but she's lived sixty years in this neighborhood and she isn't stupid. She stoops over, grabs the shaking dog, and heads for home, pronto.

From under her arm, Fatty looks back, still growling. He sees the shape move again, gathering itself into a long, thin shadow, pure black under the orange crime lights. Pure deep black.

GRACIE CARRIES THE DOG all the way up the stairs to her second floor apartment. He's heavy and makes her arm weak, but still, she hefts him up the steps. When she puts him down just inside the door of her apartment, he's still trembling all over and she reaches out to smooth the fur down along his spine. She shakes her head. "Don't know about you, dog," she murmurs. "You going senile in your old age?" She stands up, looking down at him. "Don't you dare," she says. "I got enough trouble, don't I?" She slams the door, throws the bolt, sets the chain, then hangs the leash and her jacket on the hook in the foyer. Hollers back toward the kitchen. "You got that casserole warming like I told you, Eli?"

Eli comes out into the thin hallway and nods to his mother. His pale eyes wobble in their sockets; his hair shakes with the constant twitching of his head. He leans on the wall, his long six-foot frame off balance, his weak right leg twisted. His socks slide down his skinny ankles and Gracie wants to yank them up, hard. "Yes," he says. Spit flies. He tries for more words, each one a trial: "It's good and hot, Ma." He gets the words out and smiles—sweet, sweet smile.

Gracie feels her heart ease at the sight. "That's a good boy. Go holler to Granddad, then, to get on down for dinner." She walks past him into the kitchen.

Eli tumble-walks to the doorway of the back staircase, then yells up the stairs, "Supper." Then he turns and falls into his seat at the kitchen table.

"It looks nice, son. Thank you," Gracie says, and she touches his hair. Eli's got the table set, three places, neat, like she taught him. The noodle, cheese, hamburger, and tomato sauce casserole she'd made this morning smells good and she sighs. She's home; it's okay.

She leans back out into the hall. Fatty is still sitting where she left him. He hasn't moved a muscle. He's sitting there like he froze in place, dog-lips still pulled into half a growl. "Lie down," she calls to him. "It's okay now. You go lie down."

Fatty hears the soft home tone of her voice and, slowly, his throat loosens and his fur settles down. He goes to his cushion, shoved up cozy next to the radiator in the front room. He circles, three four five times, sighs, tucks his sharp nose under his truncated tail, and goes to sleep.

JACK IS SHAKING HIS HEAD, listening to Gracie's tale of Fatty's strange behavior on the street. "Might be a coyote in the alley," he said. "I read that they're all over the city now. Creeping round where you can't see them." He lowers his voice, making it all spooky. He talks slow. "Yeah, they're out there, every night. And they're cold and they're hungry. Just waiting for prey." He reaches over fast and grabs Eli's shoulder.

"Gotcha!" he yells. He nearly falls from his chair, laughing at the terror in Eli's face.

Gracie rights Eli's toppled glass of milk and wipes up the spill with the roll of paper towels she always keeps on the table. "Now you stop that." She shakes her head at her father, but she's smiling. "Don't you go getting him all riled up or he'll never sleep tonight." She takes a bite of noodles, liking the silky slide of Velveeta on her tongue, getting just the right touch of meat. She follows up with a nice bite of bread, soft white bread folded in half, the butter warm in its center.

Eli's open mouth drains orange sauce and spit onto the table and Gracie wipes it up. "Chew, baby," she says.

Jack chuckles. "Ain't a night for sleeping," he says. He leans back in his chair and eases his half-a-leg on the other chair he's got it propped on. That's what he's always called it, what's left after his accident at the railroad yard where he worked for nearly fifty years. He's over eighty now and sharp, still. Doesn't get out much winters, but he's a help to Gracie in the house, watching over Eli days when she goes to work at Motor Vehicles, three blocks down the hill. And the building itself, where they live, he owns it, free and clear. They rent out the street-level apartment

and even the ratty basement rooms; Gracie and Eli live on the
second floor and Jack takes the top floor. He likes the view from
up there, he says, even though it's a hell of a climb up those steep
back stairs with his walker. But once he's up there, it's worth it.
He spends sunny days in his window, watching the street. Better
than TV, he always says. Better show than what they put on those
TV stories. He doesn't mind that the neighborhood's sunk so
low since he brought his red-haired Irish bride to the building,
sixty-some years ago. He sees it as interesting, a circus of sorts,
staged for his entertainment, right outside his windows.

Of course, he doesn't have to go out in it, does he? And
Gracie does. Every day—to work, to the Price Chopper for the
food that keeps all of them alive, to the CVS for the drugs that
soothe Eli's seizures, to the sidewalks to exercise the little dog
she's had for eighteen years. But, really, she doesn't mind all the
going out, not all that much, anyway; it's her life, that's all. It's
what the good Lord gave her: a son born wrong somehow, all
twisted and shaky. A husband who left, when that shaking little
baby wasn't more than three months old. A good, sweet mother,
gone now, dead, how long? Oh, a long time. A mother who died
of a heart attack twenty years ago, when she was just the age that
Gracie is now. Just sixty-two, fell over in the street, arm flung
over the curb, oranges from her grocery bag running away down
the gutter, bright orange on the gray stone. Gone.

So Gracie took over everything. Gracie is needed. And it's
hard, sometimes, being so needed. She worries—what will happen
to Jack and Eli if she fails, if she falls, somehow, along the way?
It's a burden, being so needed. But it's a life, isn't it? That's all it is.
And she doesn't really mind. Except when those mean-mouthed

songs get in her head: *motherfucker, motherfucker, bing bang boom.*

She shakes her head and looks over at her father. His eyes are almost lost in the net of wrinkles around them, but the eyes themselves are bright. "Why not, Daddy?" she says. "What's wrong with sleeping tonight?" She tilts her head and covers one of Eli's hands with her own. "And don't you go telling some story that'll scare this boy."

Eli closes his eyes and sways in his chair, humming.

"Naw. Not me." Jack smiles, his teeth yellow and chipped. "It's just that you'll want to stay awake to see the blood moon." He leans toward Eli, leering. "That's right, boy. A blood-red moon."

Tears start to roll down Eli's cheeks and he turns toward Gracie, eyes still shut. "Mama," he says. "Mama?"

Gracie stands up, a hand on Eli's shoulder. She can feel the tremor just under his skin. She knows that if it gets much worse she'll be picking him off the floor later tonight, trying to hold his head steady so he doesn't choke. She looks hard at her father. "I told you," she says.

Jack shakes his head. "Shoot. I'm sorry, honey. I shouldn't, I know. But it's hard—I forget. He's a grown-up man, Gracie. I forget." Jack lowers his half-a-leg from the chair and grabs his metal walker. He pushes himself up and then bends over Eli's chair. "I didn't mean a thing by it," he says. "It's just an eclipse, son. That's all it is—just a shadow over the moon, is all." He straightens and looks at Gracie. "And it is something you got to see, they said on the weather report. So you put this boy to bed and then come on up to the sewing room. They say it's something to see."

AND IT IS, REALLY. The moon slims down, inch by curvy inch. It's a full moon at first and it's bright, even in the orange-lit sky over the city. It's a bright white-blue and then it gets bitten into by the shadow and it darkens and darkens.

Gracie sits on the floor in front of her father's chair, looking out the window. It's one of the finest windows in the house. It's a big window, with clear beveled glass in its lower portion and stained glass along the top, a row of pink seashells in a swirling sea of foamy green. Bright sky-blue above the green, bars of red cutting through the blue. Gracie's mother used this room for a sewing room, years and years ago. She called this window the window of Heaven and Earth. Earth, she told the child Gracie, pointing out the clear glass at the street below, dusty and brown. Heaven, she added, pointing up to the colors above, spun with sunlight.

Now, moon is losing its light, high above both Heaven and Earth. Gracie sighs, leaning her head back on her father's good knee. The old man strokes her hair, her short gray hair, more bristle than curl these days. His hands smell like tomato sauce. She watches for a long time. It's beautiful and strange, but her eyes want to close now. She's seen enough. "I think I'll go off to bed, Daddy. I'm tired," she says. And she is. Tired. She works half days on Saturdays and even that half day has worn her out. Anyway, she's often tired; her legs feel like lead, sometimes, and her neck aches. Her heavy arms pull at her shoulder joints and she feels the pain shoot like a comet across her back, on and off through the day. She starts to push herself up from the floor.

Her father's hands weigh warm on her skull. "No, not yet," he says. "You just wait. The paper says that it'll turn red, just after eight o'clock." His voice is full of excitement. "I wasn't making that up, dolly," he says. "It's dust or something, in the atmosphere. Smoke from those fires out west, maybe. I wasn't lying. They call it the blood-red moon." He pushes gently on her head. "Now, that's a thing worth seeing."

And it is. For just a few minutes, the moon glows deep red. Clouds skim across the eerie light and it's one of the best sights Gracie has ever seen.

Downstairs, Fatty curls on his cushion. He's not allowed upstairs, he knows that. When Eli is sleeping, it's Fatty's place to stay on this floor with him. It's Fatty's job to yap if Eli falls. It's Fatty's job to let Gracie know; that's all he has to do. Just yap, a silly small-dog sort of noise. So that Gracie will come and hold Eli in her big soft arms, singing softly into his ear. Gracie will always come to help Eli, if Fatty just lets her know.

But Fatty has a hard time listening for Eli tonight. His heart is trembling in his chest, beating loud in his ears. He's been dreaming, short legs running and running in his sleep. He wakes up and hears, far away and low, a whole world of howling. Somewhere, out in the world, wolves and dogs are howling at the bloody moon and he feels it, deep deep deep in his own throat.

And he's worried. It's a strange night. Things are moving, out there in the dark. Fatty knows what he saw and what he smelled and what he heard, out there in the street. It wasn't a coyote. It was Death and it was reaching for Gracie.

The dog lies still but his fur rises, all by itself, prickling up and down his spine. Fatty Lumpkin knows what he knows. And he's scared.

Two

There's been a thaw at last, after three frozen months of winter. December, January, February—ice coated every sidewalk. Every day, Gracie and Fatty slithered and slid around the snow-banked blocks, morning and evening. Jack never left the apartment. Eli either. They were all getting cranky, little bits of nastiness cracking like whips in the dry apartment air. Eli got one of his terrible coughs, wracking the walls with his noise. Gracie even yelled at him once: "Shut up, shut up, shut the fuck up." It has been a hard winter.

But this March morning, the air turns soft. It's a Sunday, her day off, and early. Gracie snaps on Fatty's leash with a happy click. They stand on the front stoop of their building, the sunshine nearly blinding Gracie as well as Fatty. The filthy snowbanks along the sidewalks are melting; the gutters rush with water.

As she walks along the wet sidewalk, Gracie can hear the snow-melt pulsing through the sewer drains under the city. She stands still for a minute, letting Fatty stick his nose into some damp, earthy spot. She knows that he can feel the spring coming, too. The dirty city winter is over. It's heading downhill to the Hudson. It's washing out to sea. Gracie steps along briskly, giving up the mincy little walk she's used on the ice for months. She lets her legs stretch and she and Fatty march right along. She settles her wool hat over her ears, raises her head and sniffs at the air. Yes, yes—there's something green in this air. There is.

FATTY FEELS THE SICKENING slickness of black ice under his feet one second before she does, because he's ahead of her, tugging on his leash. His nails skitter on the ice. But there's no time, no time to warn her.

GRACIE DOESN'T KNOW what's happened, for a while. She felt it, that one second of "Oh no!" when her feet flew in the air and her whole body went airborne. She felt her head hit the sidewalk, felt it bounce, once. Closed her eyes, took a little nap. Woke to a wet, cold butt, lying as she was flat down on the icy sidewalk. And a terrible weight on her chest.

A terrible snarling weight. Gracie can't figure it out, exactly, but it seems that Fatty is crouched on her chest, his teeth bared, making that horrible, horrible growling noise she's heard only once before. His ears are flat back and his fur straight up. She can see every one of his back teeth, gray and slimed with age. His eyes are bulging. She can't move. She knows that her head aches and her butt is very cold. She's beginning to understand that she fell down, just like a child. How silly—she fell down. But what she cannot understand is why Fatty has gone crazy and why he's on her chest.

THE REEK IS everywhere and the shadow-man is bending over Gracie. Fatty can see him as clear as day—the crackling bones of the skull, the yellow fire where eyes should be. He is huge. He is hot—heat rises off his black robes in slips of filthy steam. He is grinning at Fatty; his bone-hand reaching out toward the scruff of the little dog's neck.

Fatty is not afraid, not now. He is enraged. He is furious. He is a fury. He is rage.

The hand gets under his collar and the fingers singe Fatty's skin. He snaps and snarls at the fingers. He gets one—hot stinking taste of tar—between his teeth and he bites down, every muscle in his body alive in his jaw. He hears a high-pitched laugh spring from the man's mouth. The finger jumps in his mouth, pulling away. He hangs on. He hangs on and on and on.

GRACIE IS TRYING to sit up, trying to push the snarling terrier off her chest. But, really, he's grown so heavy. She lies back, putting her swelling head gently back on the sidewalk. She closes her eyes. She starts to dream—and in her dream, she is young. Well, youngish, in her forties. Eli is just a little child, a sweet drooling toddler-baby who doesn't, yet, seem so slow. Not for his age, not yet. It's a hot June day and she is walking Eli in his stroller down this very street. She hears a small whimper from the alley. She stops. The sound comes again. It's a cry. Definitely a cry. She sets the brake on Eli's stroller and walks into the alley. It's dark and it smells and she's afraid that there are rats, but something in here is crying. She calls out. "Hello?" The crying sound stops, then picks up again, louder. There's a scratching now, too, a skittery scrapy sound, and a little yap. She sets her teeth against the smell and the possibility of rats and she leans over a metal garbage can where something, something is calling her. She leans into the dark can and, on the very bottom, soaked with filthy rain water, is the smallest white puppy she has ever seen. Its little head is tilted back and it opens its little pink mouth and howls. She feels her nipples tingle, just as they do when Eli cries and needs her milk. She speaks down into the can: "Look at you," she says. "Just look at you."

She reaches into the can, lifts the smelly pup by his neck. "Look at you," she whispers to him. "You are just a little white lump of lard, yes you are." She carries the puppy out to the stroller, where Eli waits, smiling when he sees her. She takes one of Eli's extra Pampers and she wraps the shivering little dog in it. She turns the stroller around and heads home, the puppy tucked inside her shirt, quivering against her chest.

Fatty hangs on

GRACIE NOTICES THAT THE SKY is very blue. She's looking right up into it and it's very very blue. There is something heavy on her chest but it doesn't much bother her.

Then a shadow blocks out the sky and, why, my goodness, there's Jack, leaning on his walker, tears running down his cheeks. "Oh, dolly," he's saying. "You hang on now, sweetie. The ambulance is coming. I called and they're coming."

She smiles at her father. She feels fine. "Hello, Daddy," she says. "Can you get Fatty off my chest?"

Jack is crouched down, holding her hand. "What? He ain't on your chest. He's right here. He's just right here." Jack points to Fatty, who is shaking and whining by his side.

Gracie is confused but it doesn't much matter, does it? As

long as Fatty's safe. But then she remembers and she tries to sit up. "Eli?" she says. "Where's Eli?" She struggles to her elbows. Her head is very big and very heavy, but she lifts it anyway. "Jesus, you didn't leave Eli alone, did you?"

Jack's big hand rests on her shoulder. "Relax. Relax, baby. Eli's all right." He shakes his head. "Eli's fine. Still blubbering but fine. A few minutes ago, that boy just started hollering—'Mama. Mama.' He was back in the kitchen, all hunkered down in a corner, blubbing and yelling. I told him to hush. But he wouldn't stop. He would not stop. And I thought, you know. I thought how you and Fatty had been out a longish while. So I went on into the front room and looked out the window and—God, girl—I saw you lying down here. So still."

Gracie still isn't sure, though, that her boy's safe. "Eli's okay?" she asks.

Jack nods. "Mrs. Donovan, downstairs, she ran up to sit with him. Eli's fine, dolly." Tears are still running down the ruts in Jack's old cheeks, but he tries to smile. "We're all just fine."

FATTY BARKS AT the siren and has to be held back from jumping through the ambulance doors. But that's just confusion, he knows that. It's just the aftereffects. He's seen the shadow-man go, lifting off into the breeze like a storm cloud, leaving only a touch of moldy, ashy stink behind him. Fatty's jaw aches from holding on. He thinks he feels a tooth loose in his mouth. He lets himself be led home by some neighbor or other. He lets Mrs. Donovan wipe down his wet coat and he lets Eli cry into his neck, for just a minute. Then he goes to his cushion and he curls up. But he won't sleep. He will not let himself sleep until Gracie comes home. His blind eyes sag shut. But he isn't sleeping. Not really.

Three

A FORTUNATE FALL, THAT'S WHAT ONE of the doctors called it. Because when they were taking care of her bloated head and telling her about concussions, they also listened to her stuttering heart and they took her blood pressure and then all sorts of things happened, fast: people ran around and her stretcher flew down hallways and the ceilings of the hospital sped by her astonished eyes.

And, now, in sweet warm May, Gracie has been back home for a month. She's been a little swimmy in the head and can't remember all of that month, but things are clearing up now. Sometimes, the colors come back, circling around her brain in stinging blasts of purple, red and yellow. Sometimes, her left eye still sees everything green, just before a curtain of black moves across that eye and closes out the world.

But she's much better, really. Inside her chest, a little something is keeping her heartbeat strong and steady. *Bing, bang, bing, bang.* Smooth and steady and sweet. And, best of all, she still has two more weeks before she has to go back to work. So she can just sit here in the sunshine in the front room, all day if she wants to. She can lean out the open window here and watch Earth go by. Eli's learned to walk Fatty all by himself, although Jack only lets him go as far along the street as Jack can still see from the upstairs window. Eli is very proud of his walks, even though Fatty is slow and pokey and doesn't even seem to want to sniff much. All Fatty wants to do is get back home and sit by Gracie's feet, sharing her band of sun.

Mrs. Donovan has been leaving casseroles and pound cakes, nearly twice a week. Jack has been calling cabs and going to Price Chopper, on his own. Even the silent basement tenant, Mr. Schwartz, has brought up some food—hot dogs with thick, tough skins that have to be peeled off so Eli won't choke on them.

SO GRACIE SITS in the sun, in the warm air that swirls in her open window. She waves to her father as he climbs into the cab. Then he steps back out and yells at her, "Don't you let that boy take that dog out, now. Not until I come home. Hear me?"

She hollers back. "No, Daddy, I won't. Don't worry." The sound of her own loud voice bounces around in her head. She sees the edges of greenish-black creeping toward her left eye, but she doesn't worry about that anymore. The doctors said it would go away, once her poor brain healed.

She leans her head back on the chair cushion and listens to Fatty's deep snores at her feet.

ELI'S CRIES WAKE HER. And Fatty's frantic yips. Fatty is standing on his hind legs, his tail curled under his chunky butt. He's yapping away, paws on the windowsill, scrabbling to get out. Gracie stands up. She's dizzy, as she always is when she stands too suddenly. She leans out the window. Eli is crouched on the curb, half a block down. A bunch of boys is around him. They're throwing stones. One has a big stick. Another has a cigarette lighter. He lights it, a big blue flame, and he waves it under Eli's nose, laughing.

Gracie's hand clutches the windowsill. She yells. "Hey," she screams. "Hey, you."

The boys don't even turn. But Fatty, Fatty has clamored up onto the window sill. Fatty has leapt down to the street. Gracie sees one of Fatty's fat little legs crumple when he lands but she also sees that he stands right back up, running. Running toward the boys, running toward Eli.

FATTY HAS BEEN A FOOL. He sees that now, as the stoops and little rickety trees of his street fly by him. He's been deluded. He's been snapping at shadows all this time, when, really, the danger is human and real and smells like a bunch of sweaty boys with not enough to do. His ears tell him where Eli is; he can't see anything but gray haze but his ears and his nose know where he has to be. He flies. That little fat dog really flies.

GRACIE IS OUT on the street, hollering after Fatty, screaming at the boys. She can hear Eli, yelling, "Mama. Mama."

She blasts down the street, her strange new heartbeat steady and calm, her strange new vision green and black, swirling like smoke in the air. She grabs the nearest boy. "You leave him alone, you motherfucker," she says, low and deep, in her throat, like a growl. She takes his skinny, hard little arm and tosses him backward. "Don't you touch my baby." Fatty latches himself to the boy's bare ankle.

One of the other boys, the one with the stick, laughs out loud. "Now looky here," he says. "Listen to the mouth on this old bitch." He raises the stick, a slow easy swing, and brings it down on Gracie's skull.

She puts her hands to her head, then takes them away. They're sticky with blood. She should, she thinks, have worn her wool hat. It's what the doctors said had saved her the last time. They'd also said that she must not hurt her head, not again. Again and her brain wouldn't heal. Brains don't, they said, the second time around. Not at your age. She raises her bloody right palm and smacks the boy straight across his face.

Now they all turn to her. They forget all about Eli.

She doesn't. "Run home, baby," she says, fast. "Run home. Now."

Eli runs.

The boy with the lighter swings around. He takes Gracie's shoulder in his grip and holds the flame under the ragged collar of her old cotton shirt. "You gonna burn, granny," he says.

FATTY IS CONFUSED. He's put his teeth into human flesh for the first time in his life and he's tasted human blood—like pig blood, exactly as you'd expect—and so he thought he'd done the right thing. But then everything changes.

The shadow-man is there. The boys, they're just little flares of sooty ash; the man is a looming inferno—huge, fiery. He's laughing and laughing, his voice so high that only dog ears can catch it. His great black arms are encircling Gracie and his breath licks her neck. Where the breath touches her, Fatty sees the skin blister. He hears Gracie scream.

FATTY LEAPS. HE FLIES higher than a terrier has ever flown, ever. He leaves his beloved earth, his *terra firma*, behind. He leaps. He sets his teeth in the cheekbone of the midnight man. He locks his jaw and he hangs on.

The man backs away from Gracie, screaming in anger. He raises a clawed hand and bats at the tiny white dog clinging to his face. He hisses, speaking a strange sibilant language.

But Fatty understands every word he says: "All right, then, dog," he says. "I'll take you instead." Fatty understands and Fatty is glad. He's always been glad, as long as Gracie and Eli and, yes, even old Jack—as long as his people were okay. He's glad.

Fatty feels himself lifted. He feels the black stinking wings lift beneath his little white feet. The wings are leathery. Rodent wings—he *knew* he'd smelled a rat! The wings unfurl like sails and Fatty feels the rush of air under his belly. The air grows colder and colder, the higher he goes. There is still something of spring in it, but it's fading. Fatty sets his jaw, tighter. He hangs on. Hangs. On.

IN THE SOFT MAY EVENING, after the sirens have faded and the sun gone down, things are very still. Gracie sits in the window, her shaved head stitched, her burnt neck soothed with ointment and wrapped in clean gauze. The doctors have told Jack that her wounds are not serious, that her brain is okay. Just a scalp wound, they say, this time. They've shaken their collective heads in wonder. "She's one tough old broad," Jack hears one of the younger doctors whisper to another.

The other doctor, a small red-haired intern with the lilt of Ireland in her voice, so like Jack's mother that he has to gulp back his tears, smiles. "Oh, yes. That one's got an angel on her shoulder, hasn't she just?"

But Jack hasn't proven so tough. Like Eli, he's been sedated and put to bed. It's really been more than he can bear, the way Gracie is rocking and rocking by that window, holding Fatty, wrapped in a clean blue towel, on her lap.

It is much more than anybody can bear—or believe. A bloody miracle, Mrs. Donovan whispers, as she tucks Jack into bed. It's a bloody miracle.

FATTY STIRS. HE SMELLS where he is. With Gracie. Home. He sighs. He's missing four teeth. His broken front leg aches. But it will heal. They've got it in some kind of thick plastic wrapping, something he can't chew through. It will heal.

It broke, the vet said, with a nice clean snap. When he'd leapt out the window, surely.

Fatty lowers his head, nuzzling into Gracie's lap. He knows what he knows. His leg didn't snap in that little jump. Oh no. He closes his eyes and remembers: hanging on to the cheek of the burning man. Hanging on for dear life. But that life not his own. No. Not his own.

He remembers the surprised sort of snort the man made, when he realized how happy Fatty was. How glad to be the one taken, instead of the one left behind. Then the swift flip of a leathery wing, the claws on its end tearing Fatty from his bony face.

He remembers the voice, hissing like snakes in his ear as he fell, floating free, out of the black sky, back into the sunshine, back toward Earth. He remembers what the voice said: "Next time, little dog. Next time."

GRACIE RAISES HER HAND, gently rubbing between Fatty's ears. She smiles. She didn't see it all, of course. But her strange, green-edged, blackish vision saw some of it. Enough. She saw Fatty lifted away, carried off in a great blast of smoke. She watched him go, tears running down her singed neck. But she also saw him come back. She watched. She listened to the footsteps of the boys running away, and she watched as Fatty plummeted back to her. She tried to break his fall, but she couldn't quite. She did, though, catch just a bit of his scruff in her hands, just before he hit ground. She thinks, now, that that was enough. Just enough.

NIGHT FALLS. GRACIE AND FATTY stay in the window, watching the May moon climb into Heaven. Eli and Jack sleep safe in their beds.

IN THE MIDNIGHT DARKNESS, the coyotes come creeping. They leave the alleys and they sit in the streets, rough little pairs of fur and bone and grit and guile. They raise their scrawny muzzles to the sky. They aim their eyes at the moon. There's a story to be told, and so they open up their ancient throats. Grinning, they sing.

Gigantina

O N THE VERY FIRST DAY of her life, Tina weighed in at an eensy three pounds, eight and a half ounces. That explains her name. A scrawny, screaming, seed-pip of a baby, she was put in a hot glass box and left there to ripen. And maybe that explains the rest of it? Greenhouse effect gone amok? Maybe.

ON THE NEXT to last day of her life, Gigantina could still palm the regulation-size NBA basketball her sisters had given her for her seventh birthday, wrapping her extraordinarily long and horny fingers easily around its bumpy skin. More: she could palm a whole watermelon, keeping its cool slippery green steady in her grip.

ON THE VERY LAST day of her life, it is true that Gigantina dropped the melon, but only after she'd hoisted it high above her shoulders, once twice three times, tendons trembling in her strong right hand. And, then, she had purposefully let it go, all at once, let that melon hit the ground with a liquid thud. Then Gigantina and her sisters ate its shattered flesh, picking hot pink pieces from the floor with sticky fingers, juice and tears slipping down their chins, all running together.

IN BETWEEN HER first and last days, a number of interesting things happened to Gigantina.

Growing (Way) Up

TINY BABY TINA turned into Gigantina almost overnight. At least that's what her sisters, Beth and Alice, thought. It happened when Beth, the oldest, was six; the one they all had to listen to or she walloped them, hard, if not with her hands then with her stinging words. And Baby-Alice-Blue-Eyes was three, sweet and persistent as a purple popsicle. Tina was four, brown-haired, mousy, always kind of dirty and dim, sticking her fingers into holes and sockets and who-can-even-imagine what all. The three girls were a mismatched batch but they liked each other and they played all kinds of three-girls-required games. One of their favorites involved locking arms and legs in a little circle and singing, in gleeful high-pitched voices, "Shrimp boats are coming, there'll be dancing tonight." On "night" all three girls fell backward, giggling like crazy. So they played. And they really didn't fight, much. But then, at four, Tina started to grow like some kind of out-of-whack morning glory vine—her arms took off for the sky; her legs shimmied out into long, long ropes; her neck got stringy and weak; and her head slumped permanently to her left side. Oddest of all were her fingers and toes—those digits just lit out for the territories, Beth said. (Beth was smart and had already read Huck Finn, way ahead of the pack.) Beth said that Tina's fingers and toes were going somewhere, that's for sure. Every morning, for six months, Beth put each one of Tina's out-of-control fingers into her mouth and bit down: hard snapping little bites—onetwothreefourfive, switch hands, sixseveneightnineten. Then she looked into Tina's eyes and said, "That hurt?"

Tina nodded, eyes aswim with tears.

"Good, that means they're still alive, even though they look like dead sticks," Beth said.

Alice patted Tina's back gently and said, "No, they look like little brown snakies. But that's okay." Then she plopped her plump thumb into her own pink mouth and smiled around it.

Beth did not bite Tina's toes—she just couldn't—but she believed, on logical principle, that if the fingers were alive, so were the toes.

OF COURSE, DOCTORS WERE consulted and the girls' parents took them, all three, since Tina screamed if Beth and Alice were left behind, to many a clinic and hospital and endocrinologist and rheumatologist and neurologist and orthopedist; then, eventually, off they went to healers and psychics and women with crystals in their ears and hands and eyes. And, everyone diagnosed something different, from possession by the spirit of the Ancient Oak to serotonin/melatonin/adrenaline/insulin imbalance. And none of the treatments that the family tried, from burning ritual acorns in the fireplace to pouring jars full of bitter white and yellow pills down Tina's ropy throat, had the slightest effect. So finally, when Tina was nine and Beth was eleven and Alice was eight, the parents threw up their hands and said, "Okay. So Tina's big and a bit stringy. That's all." They sighed and made the best of it, speaking with a forced and cheerful calm. "She's Big and Stringy and getting Bigger and Stringier all the time and so damn what? We love her just the way she is, don't we, girls?"

"Well, duh," Beth said, brushing Alice's shiny curls and watching Tina stretch her arms from one of the bedposts on Alice's frilly four poster to the diagonal post, easily. "I mean, really." Of course Beth and Alice loved their sister. After all, Beth and Alice had renamed Tina years and years ago. They hadn't waited for the parents/doctors/psychics to catch up—they'd done it all by themselves. Gigantina she'd become; Gigantina she'd stay. Their sister she'd always be, snug in her spot in the middle, wrapped in Beth and Alice's care. Maybe.

BUT. LITTLE GIRLS grow up, alas. Little girls grow into teenagers and that's when Embarrassment creeps into their lives, showing up as predictably as snakes in gardens. Wisely, the parents kept Gigantina out of school, so at least Beth and Alice weren't humiliated in front of their friends. And, at home, they were still all good buddies, for a little while longer.

But, one day, just looking at Gigantina's toes made Beth feel queasy and even sweet Alice couldn't, quite, meet Gigantina's eyes. And they never touched her anymore. They got busy with makeup and hair styles and, naturally, they left Gigantina behind.

And being behind was lonely. There really was no one to talk to. And no one knew, really, what it felt like from the inside, all this incessant growing. Gigantina couldn't explain it to her sisters, even if they had been listening. (Which they weren't; they plugged their ears with pop music.) Although Growth shaped her every dream and thought and extenuated molecule of being, she couldn't speak about it. In her head, though, she came up with an apt metaphor: it was like being batter poured on a too-cool griddle and running wild across the iron, forever. Her sisters, she realized, were like perfect little pancakes—rounded edges, nicely bubbled and browned, gently risen. She was amoebic. And, of course, still spreading. She never knew what direction some dribbled limb would head for next. It was disquieting. But interesting.

Taking a Lover (or Two)

THE THREE SISTERS made this crucial step out of order. The baby sister, Alice, took a lover first, at barely fourteen, just like that. Uninvited to this momentous event, Gigantina folded herself into an origami crane and secreted herself in Alice's dark bedroom closet. She watched as her baby sister's pink nipples went, one by one, into the mouth of the red-haired boy lucky enough to be in the right place at the right time, the day Alice grew tired of virginity. Just like that, lickety-split. This boy was chosen and here he was, groaning on Alice's pale-blue flowered comforter, his eyes closed, his young prick waving in the breeze. Until Alice put it in her hot little mouth, just like she'd been doing it all her life. Lick, lick, suck, suck, big moan from boy, gulp gulp gulp. Then Alice stood up and wiped a dainty hand over her swollen lips. "Next time," she said sweetly, "you have to wait until you've taken my maidenhead, all right? I'll need to see blood, right here." She ran a hand over a plump white thigh. "And there." She put one finger on his slumping penis. The boy nodded weakly. Gigantina's head felt light and airy and her legs heavy as lead, as she chewed her hard fingernails to slivers in the dark tight closet and the poor boy got ready to perform again.

When Beth the Eldest heard that Alice the Baby had been de-virginized, she was more than a little miffed. She sped up her own agenda considerably. She didn't even have a boyfriend, couldn't stand the silly, stupid high school boys in her senior class, but she found one—a chubby kid with nice gentle eyes—and she took him down, right on the living room carpet. But she was, surprisingly, more generous about spectators. In fact, she was unashamedly show-offy about the whole thing. Gigantina and Alice didn't even have to hide—Beth had invited them to sit quietly on the stairs and stare to their heart's content. Alice got bored and slipped off to her room after the main deed was done and the boy was stroking Beth's hair and telling her how much he loved her, how much he'd always admired her, how he'd been accepted by Yale, how nice her tits were, and so on. But Gigantina wasn't bored at all. She was genuinely touched. Her hands wrapped around her knees like rubber bands and some lump-like thing in her chest felt like it was trying to beat through layers and layers of brown Ace bandages. She called down the stairs, her voice screechy and hideously high-pitched, stretched (as it always was) across too-long vocal cords: "Hey, Bethy. I think he likes you."

Beth, lying on her back, her bare breasts pointing to the ceiling, smiled. The boy leapt up as if struck by arrows. His face blanched at the sight of the giant spider-girl spun around the steps. "What the hell?" he said. He turned to Beth, his backside shaking. "What the hell is that?"

Beth sat up, stretching like a happy mermaid. "Oh, sweetie, it's nothing. Nothing to worry about."

BUT. IN THEIR NEWFOUND wisdom and womanhood, Beth and Alice decided to share their delight in the pleasures of the flesh. Was this unselfish, sisterly love, in action? Or simply that, second to getting laid oneself, the next most fun thing is to get someone else laid? Or maybe they were just possessed by the typical teenage Spirit of Making Trouble? Upsetting the Apple Cart? Going One Step Too Far? Maybe. In any case, they decided that it was Gigantina's turn to lose her virginity. And, hey, Gigantina wouldn't even have to leave the house to find an appropriate male. Her sisters would do it all for her. They even gave her a choice: "Which one, G-T?" Beth had said. "Got a preference?"

Gigantina didn't take a moment's thought—she didn't need to picture the red-haired fourteen-year-old or the chunky future Yalie—she didn't need to choose. She was Bigger than any of them. She knew what she needed. Gigantina just spread herself across her king-sized bed and said, "Both, please. At once."

Alice nodded, very serious. "Righto, G.," she said. "After all, you are a double-dip handful, I'd say."

And, tactfully, both Alice and Beth went out—right out of the house, to the movies to see *Dreamgirls,* a matinee showing—while the boys spent a sunny afternoon in Gigantina's room.

So no one was there to see those two boys emerge into the twilight—both of them pale and shaken, glassy-eyed. Both of them smiling like they'd just seen the gates of heaven itself, gaping wide. Damp salty patches, pink with Gigantina's hymenal blood, stiffened the hairs on their thighs. Honey and ambrosia spilled down their cheeks.

Of course, of course. Those girls should have known better.

Because, of *course,* this act of Sisterly Sharing—or Making Trouble—caused a rift, a terrible searing rift that tore the three sisters asunder. Because neither boy would touch Alice or Beth again. All they would do was beg for those gnarled limbs and viney snaking fingers. Even when Gigantina said no, no thanks, no more. Even when the boys were almost, almost convinced that it had all been a dream. Even then, the boys wouldn't—couldn't—love perfect pancake girls, ever again. Those two boys were ruined, utterly utterly ruined. They'd been to Xanadu and they weren't coming back. Weave a circle round them thrice.

ALICE AND BETH, suddenly, were very, very afraid. And Fear, that slippery old eel, wrapped around their hearts and made them cruel. First, they taunted their sister: "Freak, freak, Freaky von Freak-Freak." Then they avoided their sister. Eventually, they just turned their pretty backs to her ugly face. They expunged her from their vision. She ceased to exist. Almost.

Dying (Fairly) Young

AND THEN THEY GREW up and left home. The two pretty sisters went away. They found homes and husbands, a Michael for Beth and a David for Alice. They moved five states away from home and three states away from one another. Soon they found babies-in-their-bellies and they tried to forget. And it worked. They played with their perfect pancake baby boys and they forgot, except in dreams, the oaken sister they'd left behind.

Well, in time, the parents died, leaving a will that left

everything they'd ever owned to Gigantina. Who, after all, they said, needed it, left all alone as she was, all alone in that big house. Alice and Beth, in their four-bedroom colonial houses far away, were separately furious and dually enraged. Their phone bills soared, as they groused to each other, nonstop: "That freaky bitch. She put a spell on Mom and Dad." But they were too afraid to say anything to Gigantina in person or by phone. They could not—would not—face her. So they chose, dually, to forget all about it. Which they did. Except in their separate snake-ridden dreams.

So Gigantina really was alone, well and truly abandoned. And lonely, yes, but not even certain about that, having no one to tell her that this mass of ice in her chest was named Loneliness. That the stone biting into her ribs was called Anger. But. Her life was interesting, still. There was always something happening, something to see, something to notice. And she never, quite, stopped growing. She'd wake from a nap to find her left big toe a quarter-inch longer, her right kneecap a smidge farther from her face. At last, when she couldn't even fit in her king-size bed, she slept on the living room floor. Right on the soft blue carpet, where her perfect sense of smell could still pick up traces of the chubby boy loving her big sister. She could spread out on the carpet, all the way out, her fingerstoeselbowskneeshipsankles spun all across the room. Life went on. If life = growth, as wise men tell us, then Gigantina's life went on, quite perfectly.

BUT, THEN, EARLY one summer morning, when she was nearly thirty years old, Gigantina had a vision. She woke up to sunshine streaming across the carpet; her head seemed suddenly to float above herself, sticking to the ceiling like an electrified balloon. From this height, this upper-region angle, she saw herself, saw Gigantina, woven into the carpet. Legs like vines, flowering; arms like tendrils, leafing. Birds in her branching hair, foxes sheltered in her dark crevices, horses running wild across the plains of her back. Gigantina's head shivered with delight—she was the most beautiful thing she'd ever seen. A pattern of surpassing beauty, she had spread to the outermost edges of the blue-carpet world. She was perfect. Divine.

Until a cloud moved across the sun and shadows filled the room. Then Gigantina's vision darkened and curdled around the edges. What she saw, then, was that she could go no farther. At the final borders of the carpet, she'd reached the farthest limits of her life. She tilted her head, sniffing at the abyss beyond. She smelled stasis; she smelled no-growth. She smelled Nothing. In the cells of her very bones, she felt Nothing growing. She knew that it was over. Gigantina was as Big as she was ever going to get. Ever. There was a shiver in her chest, as the ice named Loneliness enveloped a lung. There was a smoky hiss, as the stone called Anger cracked a rib.

Yes, for the first time, Gigantina raged. Against her fate. Against her sisters, with their husbands and their perfect pancake sons and their forgetfulness. Oh, yes, she raged, raged against the dying of the light.

And Gigantina exacted a plan. She called it Revenge and she called it Good. She took steps. First, she phoned Michael at his office and she invited him to visit his wife's family home. She told him she had Secrets to reveal. (There aren't many who can withstand such a Lure.) Michael knew nothing about her, had never even heard her name, when he came to the door, full of curiosity. When he left Gigantina's house, he dripped with honeydew; he knew everything there was to know, about this world and the next. And he could not stand to touch his wife. Beth, of course, knew where—and with whom—he'd been, the moment she saw him. She knew, she knew, she knew.

Then, Gigantina called David. It was the same thing—she wrapped him in her snaky arms and inserted her fingers into every miniscule crevice of his bodyheartsoulbrain. David left her house shivering, a veil of ecstasy flung across his eyes. Alice became invisible to him, nothing more than a troublesome shadow. And then Alice knew what Beth knew. They knew, they knew, they knew.

And Gigantina knew that they knew and it was Good, Revenge. But not quite done. Next, she made a will of her own, an invisible but fully binding will, a will that named the two baby nieces she would never see as her special heirs. She would give them what she had to give, her greatest gift: Growth. She lifted one horn-tipped finger to her lips. She bit down hard, into the tough flesh. Onetwothreefourfive switch hands sixseveneightnineten. Does that hurt, she laughed? Why, yes, my dear sisters, it does indeed. With the ten drops of blood that rose from the wounds, she inscribed her last testament into the air: *To my sister's daughters, I leave.* . . . Then she blotted her bloody fingers on the carpet—the pattern they made, two five-pointed, dark-red stars.

Her work done, Gigantina stopped eating, one lovely summer's day. She just ceased to nourish herself. She starved. She slivered down to pure bone. It was not difficult; she hadn't far to go. But still she lived. If you could call it living. No growth, nothing. So she stopped drinking, too. At first, her dry throat tormented her, day in and day out. But, slowly, slowly, her body made its peace with Nothing. Becoming Nothing, it turned out, was not so hard after all.

But there was one last thing to be done.

ON THE NEXT to last day of her life, Gigantina called her neglectful sisters, told them she was dying, and summoned them home. They must, she said, her high voice screeching over the wires, come to her deathbed. And, of course, so they must.

Frightened, sorrowful, full of loathing, they came, leaving their sons with their shadowed, ruined husbands. When they saw Gigantina, so dry, a vine without sap, something in their hearts snapped. Snapped open, with love and remembrance? Snapped shut, with utter disgust? Even they couldn't tell.

On the last day, Gigantina did her watermelon trick and the three sisters ate the flesh of the broken fruit, each piece seasoned with three sets of salt-tears. With sticky-sweet lips, The Eldest and the Youngest told Gigantina how very sorry they were. They were so very sorry; they were abject; they were ashamed. They were here, penitent, full of the truest contrition. They loved her; they always had. They begged her forgiveness. Then they asked for their husbands back. Oh, please, oh please, they said.

Gigantina smiled, licked pink juice from her gray lips and wrapped her fingers, gently, around their perfect heads. "Okay," she said. The juice ran like nectar down Gigantina's throat and, suffused with its sweetness, she died.

ALICE AND BETH, with all due speed, called the crematorium. Flames licked Gigantina's woody limbs and finally, she was Tina again, a tiny jar of ash. Nothing.

At home, the day of cremation, not knowing why, Michael woke out of his dreams and longed for Beth. David, too, awoke, shook his head, cleared his eyes, and yearned for Alice. And their wives returned. The surviving sisters mourned for Tina; they forgot Gigantina. They took their husbands into their flesh, with happy sighs. It was very nearly the perfect ending. Almost.

BUT. NINE MONTHS LATER, on a freezing March morning, Beth reached out from her bed in the maternity ward and picked up the telephone. She called Alice, who was in her own maternity ward, in her own hospital, three states away. The phone was busy, because Alice was calling Beth. This happened, over and over again.

Finally, the lines uncrossed and their voices met in the wires. It doesn't matter who said what; the message was the same: "The baby. Oh god. Ohgodohgodohgod. The baby's toes. . . ."

The telephone lines, stretched tight between two hospitals, moaned in a sudden wind. The lines crackled. The signals spit and sighed. Somewhere in the fizzing blue air, words formed. They sounded something like, "If only. . . ."

The Plagiarist

WHY?" ALTHEA LEANED TOWARD THE splotchy-pale student who sat in her small office chair, his wide khaki thighs overflowing its seat. "You had to know you were doing it. And you had to know that, this time, you'd be kicked out."

The boy's face flushed an unhealthy plum and tears began to roll down his cheeks, slowly and silently. He kept his eyes focused on his boots—they were leaking slushy, salty water onto Althea's blue rug. Ever so slowly, he nodded.

Althea flung herself back in her chair. Jesus. The poor slob. The poor stupid kid. She closed her eyes. Her heartbeat was thudding in her ears again—*boom*, boomedy, *boom*, boom, boom. Her head made it into a little song, a high whining soprano melody over the imperious bass. Then, her long training forced her to scan it: dactylic, a particularly obnoxious meter. She put a hand to her chest and coughed. Coughing, she'd read somewhere, was supposed to stop it, this runaway pounding of a deluded heart. It didn't. She coughed again. She opened her eyes.

The boy hadn't moved, hadn't wiped his tears. They were running into the woolen scarf bunched around his neck.

She leaned over her desk. "Derrick," she said. "It's so obvious."

She jabbed one finger onto the first page of his paper, right under the title he'd seemed so proud of when he submitted the paper last week, typed in bold: **The Wedding Crasher in *The Ancient Mariner*: Why You Wouldn't Have Invited Him, Either**. "Look, here are your opening sentences." She cleared her throat and read aloud, "'People got married in the nineteenth century, too, just like today. They had weddings then, too, and just like today, no one wanted weird old guys showing up and ruining their fun.'" She glanced at the boy's face; he had a small smile.

"Yeah," he whispered. "That's my thesis. I wanted to say that, you know, this guy just shows up and. . . ."

She held up a hand, palm out. "Fine. But, then, here's the next line you've written here. Now just listen." She read the words slowly: "'The ancient Mariner, bright-eyed and compulsive, is a haunter of wedding feasts, and in a grim way he is the chanter of a prothalamium.'" She stopped, letting that grand last word linger. She repeated it: "Prothalamium."

Derrick was still smiling.

Blood thudded in her neck and throat; her palm throbbed. She might have to smack him, it occurred to her. She just might have to whap him upside his dim, tear-stained, smiling, biscuit-colored cheek. Christ. She folded her hands tightly together on her desk. "Derrick, that is not you. That is clearly not your wording."

The boy nodded.

"Derrick," she said, loudly. "Listen to me."

He jumped and turned toward her, smile fading slowly away, the corners of his chapped lips drifting. His eyes were a soft spaniel brown, with no eyelashes.

None at all, she suddenly noticed. Not a lash. And very little in the way of eyebrows. No wonder he looked odd—the Pillsbury

Dough Boy. Ziggy. Was he on chemo? Oh God, a sick kid and she'd still have to ruin his life. No, no—he'd done it himself. He had cheated. Not her.

"Derrick, what's a 'prothalamium'?" She waited, knowing he didn't know. She tapped her tented hands on the desktop, in time to the beating of her blood. *Hot* diggity, *dog* diggity, *boom,* boom, boom, *boom,* boom, boom.

The damp shoulders rose and fell, once. His eyes went back to his boots and the white-rimmed puddle gathering around them.

She sighed and picked up a book from her desk and flipped to the page she'd marked with a hot pink sticky note. "It's a wedding song. The word comes from the Greek, Derrick. Greek. You might have looked it up. If you were going to plagiarize, you might have been just a bit smarter about it." She pointed to the page and the penciled star she'd made on it. "It's not your sentence, Derrick. It's Harold Bloom's sentence. See? Here it is, exactly, word-for-word, page 201, last paragraph, right here in Bloom's quite famous book on the Romantic poets. *The Visionary Company.* Really. It is quite famous, Derrick. The kind of books professors have read. Did you never think of that?"

His head rose and his eyes widened. "No," he said. "I didn't. I just—I just couldn't say it like he does. I mean," he stopped and smiled again, whispering, "the chanter of a pro-thal-a-mi-um. Man, it sounds so good, when he says it. And when I say something, it sucks. Right? I don't have enough words in my brain or something, to work with, you know, and when I say something, it stinks."

"Well. Yes." She shook her head. "But you can't just take Harold Bloom's words, Derrick, you know that. You just can't steal words like that." She closed the book with a snap. She stared into the boy's eyes. "Why the hell didn't you just put the damn words in quotes? Why didn't you just do that, with a citation? Why didn't you do that and save us both from going through all this? I called the registrar, Derrick. You have two previous plagiarism incidents on your record—proven, documented. They'll throw you out of the university this time. You're a senior. Four years. All that money. Jesus." She felt her voice start to quaver, grow high with despair, harmonizing with the twanging of her heart. She was getting too excited, she knew it. She was getting mad and that only made it worse. But she couldn't stop asking. "Why? Why? Are you ill? Do you have some sort of—condition—that is affecting your work? A disability of some sort?"

"No," he said. One of his hands rose to his face, its bitten nails plucking at the remnants of an eyebrow. "No, I'm okay."

"Then why? Why didn't you just put the lousy words in quotes, Derrick?"

His lips started to tremble. "I don't know," he said. "I wanted to. I know it's wrong. It's stealing and it's wrong. I know that. But I wanted those words to be mine, you know? I just wanted them."

Her heart drummed against her ribs. Sad stupid little fuck. And he wasn't ill. He wasn't having chemo. He just did that thing—that tripso-trichso-thing she'd read about, where people pluck out their own eyelashes. Damn.

WHEN HE'D GONE, closing the office door gently behind him, his signature on the papers she'd drawn up earlier, confessing his crime, leaving just his salty wet spot behind on her rug, she stood up, reached under her loose jacket and shifted the weight of the portable heart monitor away from the small of her back. She swung the metal box around to her side, where she could see its digital display: time passing. Quite a thing, to keep hidden, this Holter monitor—a black square buzzing box, held by a shoulder holster affair, sprouting a forest of wires that were attached to the seven color-coded electrodes stuck to her ribs and chest. The electrodes under her breasts itched. The tape, everywhere, pulled. She tried to stretch but the wires resisted. And her heart, her stupid middle-aged, fifty-four-year-old freaked-out heart that raced for no reason, that quivered in her chest like a hooked trout, kept on and on: *hot* diggity, *dog* diggity, boom.

She checked the time. Half an hour to go: she'd had the thing on twenty-three-and-a-half hours now. She was almost free. Surely she could find something to do for the last half hour. She turned toward her computer, but then hadn't the energy to switch it on. She just sat still, watching the digital read-out on the monitor tick away the minutes.

At 12:53, she decided she'd had enough. Twenty-four hours minus seven minutes couldn't really matter—close enough for government work, as her father used to say. She pulled the shade on the office window, locked the door, and took off her jacket and turtleneck and bra. One by one, she pulled the tape away from the electrodes, wincing as it tore her skin. Then the electrodes themselves—the blue from atop her left breast, the brown from her right, and so on down to her ribs: white, green, red, black, orange. Each disengaged electrode dripped a clear, bluish goo. She found a plastic bag in her file cabinet and dropped them in. When they were all in there, sliming together in a gluey bunch, she twisted the bag into a knot and tossed it in her wastebasket. She located tissues to wipe her skin. She lifted her breasts and tried to see the skin below them, where the electrodes had been glued—she couldn't really see much but what she could was red and swollen, puffy, damaged. Everything burned. For one moment, her eyes seemed to drift up to the ceiling and look down: she saw herself standing there, a full professor of literature in her tasteful book-lined office, Althea Roland, PhD, naked to the waist, welts bubbling up all over her torso. As if she'd been attacked by wasps. Or subjected to a long, tortuous experiment by aliens. With a strange buzzing box and wires gripped in her hands. She smiled. Well. Just like poor dumb Derrick. We smile from the midst of the hopeless, hapless messes we get ourselves into, don't we, son?

Dressed again, Althea put Derrick's signed papers into her book bag; she'd make Xerox copies and bring them to the registrar's office on her way to drop off the monitor at her doctor's office. She'd told Derrick it was out of her hands now, that the process of dismissal would begin the minute the registrar got these papers, that he'd hear from the Dean shortly. All she had to do was turn in the evidence. Like a good detective, her work was done—the punishment, thank God, was not her responsibility. Oh, he'd said. Okay. He hadn't even blinked, as he'd shuffled out her door. So be it. Amen. Good riddance to a bad cheater. *Que sera, sera,* eh?

She wrapped her head in her old gray scarf and hefted the book bag, grown suddenly heavy with evidence and a Holter monitor, still faintly buzzing. God, it was a good thing she didn't have to pass through a metal detector; some half-trained university security guard would shoot her—they were allowed to carry guns these days, a terrible irony waiting to happen. She stepped out the door. But when she got outside, into the ice-slickened aftermath of the third February storm so far this semester, it was all she could do to stand up and slither her way down the sidewalks to the freshly-salted parking lot. She wasn't risking her brittle, honeycombed bones by walking the two extra blocks to the registrar's office. So the papers that would ruin Derrick's life could stay in her book bag one more day. Big deal. Fuck it.

Maybe he'd get lucky and she'd die before she turned them in—her car would slide into a tree on the slick mile between the college and the medical center. Or she'd have the massive heart attack tonight, all tucked in and cozy in her bed, then suddenly struck by the unbelievable, undeniable first pain, a granite boulder dropping onto her chest, cold sweat springing from her skin. She would thrash in panic, trying to draw in air, terrified, alone. It would hurt, horribly, but briefly. Then she would become still and very, very quiet. Her old dog, her ancient, half-blind faithful dog, her very own Argos, her old sweet dog would curl himself beside her, whining, trying to warm her cooling body. Derrick just might get that lucky, the poor shmuck. It could happen. That kind of thing happens sometimes. That kind of last minute reprieve. It does. It could. It might.

BUT IT DIDN'T. She gave the monitor to her doctor's receptionist, who tossed it casually onto the counter and said, "Here's your appointment to come talk over your results. Bye now." So she went home to her normal post-divorce-times-two routine. She ate a peanut butter sandwich for supper. She graded papers and watched television simultaneously, hoping each activity would neutralize the painful futility of the other. She went to bed and slept badly, wakened over and over by her jolting heart. But she did not die.

On Tuesday, she went to her 9:30 class—nineteenth Century

British Literature—and there Derrick was, slumped in the back row like always. She put her books down on the front desk and opened her attendance book. She checked his name off—he'd never missed a single class. And wouldn't now, apparently, although his college career was certainly over. It most surely was. There are rules: Repeat plagiarists do not graduate. Have a permanent record of cheating. Don't get a refund. Don't get a diploma. It was over. Kaput. End of story. *Fini.*

But here, after all, he was. He wouldn't speak in class—he never had. But he would take notes and use his yellow highlighter to mark the passages she talked about in his *Norton Anthology.* And when she read some poetry aloud, he would close his eyes and nod along with the beat, smiling, happy. He would. He always did. And he would, apparently, keep on doing it until someone told him, officially, that he could not. He would not leave until someone planted a big official boot in his ass and kicked, hard. No, dear Derrick would not go gentle into that good night, not at all.

Her heart dove—took a spectacular plunge into her diaphragm. Its fall left that peculiar hollowness in her chest, that empty second when there was no beat at all, that airless moment that felt like a little death—yes, and a bit like *la petite mort,* orgasm, but not really, not enough—before it thudded hard against her ribs and quivered there, trembling. Over and above all that commotion in her chest, she heard herself say calmly, "Okay, folks. Today it's Keats." She laughed a little, flipping the rice-thin pages of her heavily annotated text. "If I'm not mistaken, today we tackle Keats' sonnet, 'When I Have Fears that I May Cease to Be'."

How perfect. How stupidly divine, her timing these days.

Her syllabus = her life + her death, times X. Solve for X, the great
unknown. She sighed quietly and began to read the poem aloud,
beating along in fine iambics, her voice strong and steady, far out
of sync with her crazy heart: *When I have fears that I may cease to
be/ Before my pen has gleaned my teeming brain.* Oh, yes, perfect.
She looked up to see Derrick's eyes closed, his face alight with
his hopeless, ecstatic listening.

ON TUESDAY AFTERNOONS, between 2 and 3, during her office
hour, Althea always e-mailed her best former student, the one
who'd himself gone on to become a professor, to teach at another
college, and so on. The one she'd been in love with but had never
told, because it was against the rules to love a student. Even
though he'd been a grown man, even then—the one-in-a-million
brilliant guy who came back to school at thirty-five, after being a
musician, a cook, a drunk, a carpenter, a clerk in the A&P. And
she'd only been forty back then, herself: not so much older. A
new professor herself, back then. Divorced, twice. No kids—she
had a PhD instead of kids, she liked to say. So he hadn't been so
very far away, so forbidden, had he? But she wanted tenure; she
couldn't take a chance, could she? So, instead of risking it, making
a damn fool of herself, she'd gotten a puppy—black and fuzzy
and utterly in love with her. The World's Best Dog, she liked to
say. And, really, he still was.

And then, like all of the good ones, the brilliant student had
graduated. He'd finished his thesis, collected his 4.0 GPA and
was gone. They'd written, for a while, then not. More than ten
years of not. Recently, she had Googled his name—no reason,
just curious. And found that he, too, had acquired what was

called a "terminal degree," as if he, too, had gotten what would be his last disease. She e-mailed; they caught up. He was chair of his department and, funny thing, he'd married. One of his own bright students, two weeks after she graduated and made an honest man of him. And he'd gotten tenure, as well.

So, she'd loved and lost in silence and the world had kept on turning, as it does. But, still, he made her laugh even now, by e-mail. His office hour was between two and three, Tuesday to Thursday afternoons. Ah, sweet synchronicity. For weeks, they'd been trading made-up slang names for English courses. She'd send a name; he'd define the course and vice versa. It wouldn't have entertained anyone else, perhaps, but it brought light to Althea's small days—somehow, it calmed her heart. It had started simply— he'd called her Literature by Women course "chick lit." She'd sent back "prick lit" for his Masculinities in Western Literature course. He'd come up with alternatives for the women's lit course: Clit lit. Bitch lit. It got less and less politically correct. She kept a list of all their course names so far; it made her chuckle to read it:

Mick lit = Irish Literature

Zit lit =Adolescent Literature

Hip lit = The Beat Generation

Stiff lit = Murder Mysteries

Swish lit = Gay Literature (Alternative: Limp wrist lit)

Crip lit = Literature of the Differently Abled

Gefiltefish lit = Jewish Literature

Whip lit = The Writings of the Marquis de Sade

Flick lit = Film Studies

E'nit? lit = The Stories of Sherman Alexie

Pip lit = *Great Expectations*

Nit Wit lit = The Benjy Section of *The Sound and the Fury* (also acceptable: Lenny's parts in *Of Mice and Men*).

HER FINGERS CLICKED over the keyboard; she'd had a brainstorm overnight, lying awake, listening to her heart sputter and chug. "Dickless lit," she typed. "Hint: it's not a whole course, just one book." She sat back and waited.

Two seconds later, his message came back. "Hard one. (Ha, ha.) Have to think about it. No time now, though. Have to fly to Maine; Gina's father died yesterday. Suddenly—only mid-fifties. Out of the blue. Stroke. Terrible timing: did I tell you we're pregnant?"

She sent back: "Oh no. So sorry. Write when you get back. When you have time." She turned off the machine and held her face in her hands. She could feel that she was flushed, that blood was pumping hard into the frail little vessels of her face. Her brain. She had tears in her eyes and she didn't know why. She couldn't be sorry that some girl named Gina, whom she'd never seen or met or wanted to know or know about or even know existed, had lost her father, could she? Hell, no. She could be furious, though—furious that he'd married someone whose father was as old as herself. Someone young enough to be pregnant. Oh, yes, she could still be furious. And she was. Oh God, she was.

ON WEDNESDAY, ALTHEA sat on the table in her doctor's examining room, paper crinkling under her. She had meant to turn in Derrick's papers on the way to the doctor, but just didn't have time. The nurse took her blood pressure, smiled, went out of the room, came back in, took it again, and went out again. Althea's heart went crazy, leaping like, like what? She thought for a minute, in search of the perfect simile. Okay—her heart was leaping like a wild deer caught in the cage of her ribs. That wasn't bad. Lines from a Marvell poem swam into her ears: *The wanton troopers riding by/ Have shot my fawn and it will die.* It was interesting, wasn't it? An early word for "deer" was "hart." Surely not coincidental? Nothing was, really, coincidental. She coughed and looked at her swinging feet; they hadn't made her take her tights off and so her feet were clad in black, with a small hole beginning on her right big toe. But that couldn't matter here—in the cardiologist's offices, they only cared about the parts from the waist up. She crossed her arms over her chest and rocked, humming.

DR. ENGLEMAN'S HAIR was reddish today, with gold highlights. It was the most astonishing thing—a cardiologist who changed his hair color weekly. It went from silvery gray to deep brown to sandy blond, a constantly changing array. It was the only odd thing about him, though. He was a tiny man, near her own age, neat and thin and gentle, with round black-rimmed glasses. Today, he shook his head and put his hand on her wrist, feeling her pulse. "Althea, your blood pressure is way up. It's horrendous. We'll have to change your medication."

"Oh. Yes, okay." She never could speak well to Dr. Engleman. She lost her training, her wit, her built-in facility with words, the minute she was faced with anyone in a white coat. "Um. What did the Holter show?"

He smiled and pulled a fat bunch of paper from her file. "Look!" he said. "If I unfolded this, it would roll across the room and all the way down the hall! Look, your heart beat 112, 782 times while you had this on." He pointed to the number at the top of the summary sheet. He giggled like a child. "112, 782 beats in one day! Isn't that amazing? What we ask that little old pump to do, every day." He leaned over and patted her shoulder. "You know, they used to think that everyone, at birth, got allotted a certain number of heartbeats and when they were gone, they were gone. Boom, your number was up. Literally. Isn't that funny?" He put a stethoscope on her back and waved a finger when she started to speak. "Shhh."

So, she just thought of what she'd like to say: Yes, I know about that heartbeat limit; that's why the poets, the sonneteers, declared that their love was killing them. If the woman they loved was so damn beautiful that she made their hearts beat fast, she was killing them, one lost heartbeat at a time. *But at my back I always hear. . . .*

He took the stethoscope away. "Your heart is going like a jackhammer, Althea. No wonder you get dizzy." He dangled the Holter report in front of her. "But there's nothing really wrong. Look." He pointed to the report. "It's fine. See? It says 'normal sinus rhythm.' Some palpitations, the kinds called PVC's and PAC's. Neither of those kills you, by the way. They're nothing—I mean, I know they might feel like they're going to kill you, but they don't. Everyone over fifty has them. You must just be super-sensitive to feel them as strongly as you do. Oh, and you also had some brief incidents of tachycardia. Tachycardia just means 'fast heart.' So, sometimes, your heart goes, like 125 beats a minute. That's fast. But then it stops, on its own. So, that's nothing, too."

She felt tears rising in her eyes.

He leaned closer, tapping her arm with the metal round of his stethoscope. "Do you understand, Althea? You're fine. I think, well, I think you just get scared. Your blood gets full of adrenaline and that fools your heart into going into 'fight or flight' mode, for no good reason. It feels like you're in danger, but you're not.

It's a fake warning. False alarm. You just get scared. That's all. We'll get you started on a new blood pressure medication and we'll recheck your heart in six months. How will that be?"

She couldn't stop the tears and words she hadn't even thought about came spilling from her mouth. "You know what, doctor?" she said. "You know what happened this morning? My dog peed blood. He's the World's Best Dog. He's 14 years old and going blind, but I still believe he'll live forever. He's got to. But then today, in the snow, he peed blood. Big red splatters. And he whined the whole time." She tried to take a deep breath, but her throat was too tight. "Of course I'm scared. I'm looking straight at mortality, every fucking day. Little skeletons dancing around my head. *Memento mori.* Aren't you scared, too? Aren't you scared spitless at least fifty per cent of the day and eighty per cent of the night, doctor? Aren't you?"

Dr. Engleman pushed a hand through his hair and backed away. He began to write in her file. "And maybe something for anxiety, too."

AT THE DESK, filling out the check for her co-pay, Althea stopped. She looked at the nurse behind the counter and said, "Do you know the term for the psychological disorder where people pull out their hair? You know, their eyelashes and all? I think it's a kind of compulsive disorder? Part of obsessive/compulsive disorder? Tripso-something?"

The nurse stared. "No," she said. "I don't. You want me to ask one of the doctors?"

"No," Althea said. "I can always look it up."

But when she got back to her office, she didn't look it up. It didn't matter, what the right word was, did it? The perfect word wouldn't change a damn thing.

Unless. . . . Unless that word was beautiful, so powerful that it did change everything. Like the words people used to believe in, long ago, words so full of power and mystery that they shouldn't even be spoken, words that summoned up the godhead or conjured up the devil. She turned the key in her car's ignition and whispered into the dashboard: "Yahweh." Nothing happened. "Beelzebub." Nothing still. She drove home slowly over icy, treacherous roads. "Bibbity bobbity boo," she sang.

ON THURSDAY, 9:30, Derrick came to class. And the following Tuesday, too. And the next Thursday, when she gave an exam, he came and took it, sweating doughily over his blue book. And the next Tuesday, when he got his exam grade back—C+—he smiled. He hadn't recognized all the quotes, but he'd identified the Keats one, hadn't he? Derrick's plagiarism papers stayed in her book bag—she still hadn't had time to turn them in to the registrar. Or the energy. She was so tired, all the time. Her heart leapt crazily, day and night. She hardly slept, afraid to be jolted out of dreams by the screeching false alarms that came knocking on her ribs like sly messengers, like telegrams from the front, like phones suddenly shrilling in the middle of the night. She didn't take her pills, any of them—not the Lotrel, not the Pravachol, not the Xanax, the Fosamax, the Miacalcin, the Caltrate, or the StressTabs. Not even the herbs: no black cohosh, no soy extract, no kava kava, echinacea, chamomile, or rue. No eye of toad or toe of newt, either. Why should she, if all she was was just scared, for no good reason? Fuck it.

Two weeks later, the vet told her that her dog had cancer in his bladder and it would be kind, soon, to put him down. But she couldn't, she knew that. She bloody well could not destroy the World's Best Dog. It was just too much to ask, wasn't it?

Four weeks went by and she didn't hear from her former, brilliant student. He had, apparently, grown weary of their silly little game. Maybe he was too busy, supporting his young wife through her first grief. Maybe she really was that young, his wife, that fragile in her present state. That new to the world of sorrow and of death.

She sent one last email: "Dickless lit = *The Sun Also Rises*. Ha. Ha. Get it?"

She never heard back.

ALL THROUGH MARCH, it snowed again and again. Every morning, afternoon and evening, her dog stained the snow red, deeper than pink now, splashes of surprising scarlet in the clean white. Often now, he cried in his sleep. Sometimes, he shuddered and groaned. Sometimes, his eyes would suddenly shoot open and wide and there he'd be, perfectly still, staring wildly into space, shivering.

One night, a bitterly cold moonlit night, she urged him into his evening walk around the block. "Come on," she told him. "We need the air." Even her city street looked lovely in the glassy blue light of moon on snow. Her two booted feet and the dog's four padded feet crunched along together in the diamond-hard snow, a kind of contrapuntal harmony.

But then, about halfway round, the dog simply sat down. He lowered his butt onto the ice and just sat. She tugged his leash, gently. "Come on, sweetie," she said. "Let's go home." He sighed, and lowered his front half to the ice. He stretched out like a flat black dog-shaped shadow, right there on the sidewalk. He closed his eyes.

Her heart flipped in her chest, then sank, fluttering and skittering against her ribs. Oh God, not here. Not now. She crouched down beside him. She held one of his silky-cold ears in her mittened palm. "Oh, please," she said. "Come on." His tail wagged once, but he made no effort to stand.

She knew she couldn't lift him, couldn't carry his weight in her arms. She held tightly to his ear and lifted her face to the winter sky, a silent plea, as close to prayer as she could get. The night was still. Nothing.

Althea slid down on the sidewalk and wrapped her warmth around the old, tired dog. She lifted his ear and whispered into it, the first thought that hit her brain: "Once," she said, "there was a poet named Elizabeth Barrett—yes, yes, later she married Robert Browning and became Elizabeth Barrett Browning—that's the one!—and she had a dog named Flush, a dog she loved with all her heart. Flush even got dognapped once, you know, and Elizabeth, who was an invalid, left her bed to save him. She and her lady's maid traveled into the terrible slums of London, all alone, two trembling, respectable Victorian women and they got Flush back. Elizabeth's brothers wouldn't go; her father wouldn't. It was silly, they said, so much fuss over a dog. But Elizabeth and her maid went. They gathered their little bits of money and they paid the ransom and they saved him. They did!" Her lips were numb now and she was beginning to slur her words, but she kept talking. "Oh, yes, it's all true. Later, long after Elizabeth and Robert and Flush were dead and gone, Virginia Woolf wrote a book called *Flush*. Did you know that, sweetie?"

The dog's tail gave another slow thud against the ice, so she went on, her voice misting the air and coating the dog's ear with frost: "Yes, and this is what the book says, how Woolf quotes Barrett, who is describing Flush. This is how it goes." Althea closed her eyes and pictured the page in the book she was teaching in her Senior Seminar. Pages glowed in her head; she could read the words right off the back of her eyelids, like magic. "Yes, I've got it. Listen: *He was of that particular shade of dark brown which in sunshine flashes 'all over into gold.' His eyes were 'startled eyes of hazel brown.' His ears were 'tasseled'; his 'slender feet' were 'canopied in fringes' and his tail was 'broad.'* She opened her eyes. "Isn't that lovely?" She sat up, her arm around the dog's shoulders. "Come on, now. It's time to go home. I'll tell you the rest at home. It's a good story. In Italy, Flush fathers puppies and Elizabeth—in her late forties!—has a son. Really! You'll want to hear how it all turns out. Come on."

Slowly, the dog's head lifted. With a great sigh, he pushed himself into a sitting position. Althea tugged his collar and he tottered upward until he could stand. Together, under the icy moon, they limped their slow way home.

THE NEXT MORNING, she called the vet's office and made the appointment, for the first day of winter break. The cheery voice of the young assistant fell into somber tones when she realized what the appointment was for.

Althea wrapped the telephone cord around her arm like a blood pressure cuff, looking at the calendar on the kitchen closet door. "He hates coming to the office," she said. "He gets so scared. Is it possible for someone to come here? He's been your patient for fourteen years and so I thought that perhaps. . . ."

"Wow. Fourteen years." The girl's voice slipped back into cheer, despite herself. "I've only been here, like, three months. But I'll ask the doctor. I think she'll come out to your house. She does, sometimes, for, ummm, you know, that sort of thing."

Suddenly, Althea felt the urge to giggle. "Of course she does," she said. *"Because I could not stop for Death—/ He kindly stopped for me."*

"Excuse me?" the girl said.

"Nothing. Poetry. Nothing." Althea pressed her hand to her chest, staring at the calendar. She wouldn't mark it down, that appointment. That was just too much to ask—she would not write those words in her kitchen.

ON THE LAST Thursday before spring break, she took the plagiarist's papers out of her book bag and, after class, she called him to her desk. He stumbled up, pale as oats. She held out the papers. "Take these," she said, "and do whatever you want with them. I won't say anything, either way."

He blushed, right up to his bald eyelids, his skin turning a soft, creamy peach. "I—what?"

She leaned over, speaking gently. "Surely you remember 'Dover Beach': *neither joy, nor love, nor light, nor certitude, nor peace, nor help for pain.* All of us, all the time, we're all just dicking around on this goddamn darkling plain. You see? There's really nothing to be done, Derrick, nothing at all. Take them."

He took the papers from her hand, then backed away.

"Oh, wait," she said. "You'll be so pleased. I just thought of this, just this morning and I wrote it down, right here, for you."

She smiled at him, holding out the piece of paper where she'd jotted the magic word, just as it had come to her in the icy dawn as she sat stroking her old dog's silky head. *Trichotillomania: From the Greek. Tricho = hair. Tillein = pull. Mania = madness.* "Take it, Derrick. It's your word. It's perfect and it's for you."

The boy's hand plucked the piece of paper from her fingers and shoved it in with the others. He gripped the whole dog-eared mess against his chest. "I have to go," he stammered. "I have another class."

She nodded. "Of course. Just don't forget to read that, Derrick. It will make all the difference." She stood up, leaning over the desk toward him. She lowered her voice. "And, Derrick, you just go ahead. Just go ahead and steal all the fucking life you can, right now." She put a hand to her pounding chest then slapped it down on the desk, hard. "Right here. If you cannot make your sun stand still, Derrick, yet you will make him run. Make him run, Derrick."

The boy backed farther away. He backed all the way to the classroom door and into the crowded hall, where he was swept from her sight, still clutching his papers.

Funny. He hadn't seemed comforted, not at all, not as she'd expected. He hadn't looked saved or even grateful, the dumb cluck. Not one bit. No, what he had looked was terrified. Yes—that was it. He looked terrified, for no good reason.

Like a Virus

I. Paranoid Schizophrenia

F EAR INFECTS, THAT'S WHAT I hate about it. You see it, all red and teary, in some poor sucker's eyes and then, before you can clap a mask over your mouth, sure enough, it's crawling around on all of your mucus membranes, too. A virus. It climbs inside every soft, pink, damp spot you've got: spit dries, lungs crackle, guts heave and, oh yes, assholes tighten (or worse, loosen).

That's why I just do not want to let this woman step over my threshold and into my house. I can see it right through the thick old glass of the door. She has fear leaking around her eyes, leaching all the fake happy out of her smile. But, you know, that's the other thing about the fearful—they smile so pretty and they kind of plead without saying a goddamn thing and before you know it, they're standing in your living room, holding out a plate of warm brownies. And saying, "I moved in next door last week." And her eyes go fidgeting all around her face and you know, you just know, that you should take her and her brownies (from a mix, you can always tell by the smell—overly sweet and funny with some chemical pretending to be butter) and throw them straight out of your house. Know you should glare like the neighborhood madwoman, just go ahead and crank her fear up a notch, can't hurt her any more than she's been already, and turn her away, for everyone's own good.

But that's not possible, is it? So I smile my own sad smile and cough a few times, trying to shoot her infection out of my throat, and I say, "Well. That's nice. In the upstairs apartment?" I hold out my hand, palm up, all bare, exposed like the wide open mouth of some baby bird, and into it slides the plate. It's paper, already soggy on the bottom.

She looks like she'll pass out from pure gratitude, so what I don't say is what I know about the old lady that had that apartment up until last month and how she died in there all alone and got hauled out at last by a bunch of guys with handkerchiefs over their noses. It was late May, and warm. And how I watched from my bedroom window and so I saw the whole sorry scene framed in the colors and shapes of the stained glass in that old window and how even with that to inspire me I hadn't a prayer to say for her lonely old soul.

Nope. I don't say that, who would? I say, "Come on into the kitchen, then. I bake on Thursdays and there's dough rising." And there is, although from the look of her and her box brownies, she wouldn't know that bread has to set and rise and doesn't just come sliced and dressed in plastic bags, all red and blue and slippery.

She puts her skinny rump into one of my oak chairs (only two left from a set of four—things fall apart) and runs her hand over the tablecloth. "Smells good in here," she says.

I nod, putting on the kettle and slipping two tea bags into mugs. I set the limp plate of brownies onto the table and she smiles again—I'm going to have to eat one, I can see that. So I get it over with as fast as anybody could, swallowing it damn near whole. Even so, I could choke on the aspartame alone. These are, then, diet brownies of some sort. It's enough to make a person cry, the things that people worry about—good clean sugar never hurt you, I promise. I bake all my own sweets, out of pure butter and sugar and milk and real eggs and I'm fine, right? For fifty, pretty near fine, anyway.

And then, she never even eats one herself. Instead, she starts right in, spilling fear all over my kitchen. She looks at me with her jumping blue eyes and, I swear, just like she went to school to get this exactly right, took sociology classes and Psycho 101, studied up on paranoid schizophrenia and then practiced her lines, she says, "They followed me from my old apartment and they're looking at me at night from the school across the street. The janitor lets them in, he's in on it, you know, the fat creepy blond one? They stand there in that dark classroom on the right-hand corner and they look into my windows. One night they sat in their car and shined their headlights right up into my bedroom window, all night. Lights made big circles on my wall and I had to lie flat in bed so they couldn't see me take off my clothes." She stops to take a ragged little breath. "I just thought you ought to know." She bares her teeth and I think I'll hear some sort of horrible growl, but she's pointing to her teeth. They're all brown around the edges, soft and crusty. "My mouth hurts. I can't go to my dentist anymore," she says, "because they follow me and get into the waiting room and stay there, waiting until I'm knocked out with that gas or something and can't yell. So I can't let the dentist give me anything for pain, and then I just can't stand it." She leans back in her chair and closes her awful mouth.

The tea kettle is screaming. I get up, pour water into the cups and dunk bags, up and down, up and down. There's not much use in even trying, is there? But hell, when I bring the cups over, steaming nice and warm into the yeasty air, I say, "How did they get the headlights to point *up* like that?"

Of course she doesn't answer that. She just holds her mug in two hands. I can see that her hands are cold—that's another thing fear does, it sucks blood from the extremities and sends it all to the vital innards and big muscles like thighs that don't do you a damn bit of good when you're sitting down and who has any choice of position when you get scared?—and that she'll use the tea to warm her blue fingers but never take a sip, because she can't put anything that's been made by a stranger into her mouth, not her, she's too clever for that old trick. So she cradles that mug like a baby in its bath and she says, "They follow me to Price Chopper, too. I used to work at the one downtown, the one by Lark? And I had a little trouble with my supervisor, you know, and I think she told them where I live now, and now, I can't go to any Price Chopper in the whole city and it's expensive to buy food at the little store on the corner."

Well, she's right, it is. I know that, since I have them deliver all my groceries, only place left in the city that delivers anymore. And I try not to eat anything from a can or a box so, believe me, it is expensive. I nod and take a sip of my tea. It's hot but feels good, burning those fake brownie chemicals out of my throat. "I'll bet."

That makes her happy. She stands up, a little blond girl with wrinkles around her eyes already and hands that won't stop shaking even now that we've warmed them up. "Well, I thought you should know. You'll keep your eyes open, won't you?"

I smile. "Sure I will. Always do." I stand up, signaling her that it's OK to leave.

She backs out of the kitchen and all the way down the hall. She faces me as long as she possibly can—too smart to leave herself open to attack from the rear. When she finally spins out the doorway, I feel like I *could*, you know. Throw something heavy or send a bullet into her skinny little undefended spine. Like I should, really. Just to make her feel better, show her she's been right all along.

II. Agoraphobia, Squared

B UT WHAT I do is, I start watching her. I have a perfect view of the street from my upstairs windows, a kind of wide panoramic view of everything that happens on this one little block. The old Victorian daddies who built this house understood something about watching, I think. Their women stayed inside, mostly, and at least they understood that it was wise to give the ladies something to watch and even to surround it with these pretty borders of stained-glass flowers and shells and wreaths and whatnot. As if the scenes from the street were framed, like the pictures on the walls, like dried ferns under glass. And pictures never hurt you, did they? No harm there. All the houses on this street used to hold families who looked out windows and kept watch over one another. Now the houses are all cut up into little rabbit-hole apartments, the old carved oak paneling ripped apart to make new walls and doors, kitchens stuck in the oddest places, toilets any old where. Except my house—mine is still whole, thanks to my very own Daddy, not quite a Victorian but just as dead.

So, anyway, I start to watch particularly for her. But, of course, she's clever. She keeps to no routine and she sort of darts in and out of her house, holding herself sideways, presenting a narrow target. I just get a glimpse now and again. Sometimes, she waits until that funny time of the day, just at dusk, to go out. That time when the streetlights haven't flipped on yet, when the sky still hangs onto some light but doorways darken. She's like a bat, loving that time of day. And hell, our streetlights don't even come on, half the time. Shot at by rocks and weighted by who knows how many pairs of tied sneakers, rotting there in our air, swinging away up there until the laces decompose enough to let gravity do its work. Why do they do that, kids? You'd think they'd need those damn expensive sneakers, wouldn't you? Where are their mothers, that let them get away with that kind of waste? Anyway, she slips out into that no-color time and kind of floats down the street, head twisting over her shoulder every three seconds, like some kind of sidewalk swimmer reaching for a breath. The air gets darker as she goes, erasing her wake.

And, yes, I start to watch for people watching her, too, can't help it. I know the fat creepy janitor who works at the school across the street and I hate him myself, on looks alone, but I have to admit that I never catch him leading tour groups through the school to go stare into her windows. Neither do I see cars full of men with binoculars, levering their vehicles into acute angles so that their headlights point straight up to the second floor, directly into her window. I almost wish I did, it would be interesting. I imagine that you could, with some work and planning, jack up the front end of your car almost high enough to do it. But it would take some understanding of physics and angles and I don't see anyone around who looks like a geometry teacher. Our block runs to ranging mobs of fifteen-year-olds with pit-bull puppies they're raising to be just as vicious and hurtful as themselves. Puppies with skinny little whip tails and big jaws and skittery eyes. But these kids don't pay any attention to the nervous little woman sidling in and out of her front door—to them, she's too old for sex and too poor to rob. And she's crazy—even the pups can smell that.

So it gets to be July. And I know she'll come over again, one of these days, but I've been busy and time's been passing. Summer is bad, sometimes. It's hot in the house and you'd like to keep your windows open but don't dare. Oh, now and again a crack during the day but never at night, when you'd really like a breath of cool air. And it's humid and things start to grow in corners: spiders, mold, things you just don't want to know about. What my mother always did in summer when I was young was this: she stretched cheesecloth over the screens and kept the windows shut, too. This kept the house kind of dim, but cool and sheltered. She believed that the cheesecloth filtered out the DDT they were spraying all over the city in those days to kill mosquitoes. Once, my mother took a red crayon and circled one line in my sixth-grade copy of the *Odyssey:* "An evil mist enfolds the world." And there we had it. No arguing with Homer. And, later, my mother could never fall asleep without making sure the toilet seat was down and weighted with a brick because she'd read someplace that rats had climbed through the sewer and straight into someone's house, coming out of the toilet all dripping and dark, their rank fur slicked back like those duck's ass haircuts my boyfriends sported. Well. There's not much to say about all that, is there? (Except to note

that, as you can imagine, my mother leaked her particular brand
of fear all over the house and it took a lot of Lysol to wash it out
after she died. And, yes, since you ask, she died upstairs in the
bedroom I now call my own, the one with the biggest window,
with the prettiest stained-glass border, but she was taken out
quick, no handkerchiefs that time, because I was with her and
knew the minute that her lungs threw out their last bit of air.
I took the heavy gauze mask from her mouth—she'd insisted,
to the last, that I keep it on her, to save me from catching her
failure of heart—kissed her lips and called an ambulance about
half a second later. Never hold on to things that can't be saved.)

It's a hot July night when the woman comes back. It's late.
She's too smart to ring the bell, because that might rouse the whole
neighborhood and then they'll know that she's out on the street all
alone—well, on my porch, really, but still exposed. So she starts
to call my name, aiming her squeaky little voice up toward my
window. (I've never told her my name, so she must have stolen
a look at my mail or something. She is a little minx, isn't she?
And clever. She has to be.) "Anna," she says. "Anna Rose, please."

I wake up right away. Maybe I wasn't really asleep, anyway,
maybe just lying in a sweaty half-dream. Because I feel like I've
been expecting her and her voice sounds as familiar as can be:
exactly the sort of high-pitched sound that you get out of a throat
that tight, its soft pink membranes all abraded and stiff.

"Anna Rose! You've got to let me in. They're in my house."

I sigh. They. It's always they, isn't it? Always plural and non-
specific. My mother's favorite, "they," wasn't even human: it was
chemical. Poison on the fruits. Death in the air. Radiation. For
the last ten years of her life, she only ate food from cans, nothing
fresh. I can still choke, just thinking about tinned asparagus, slimy

and stringy and threading apart on the tongue, tangling in the throat like tiny green snakes.

"Please, Anna. Please." A stone hits my window. Just a little one, but still.

I get up and walk down the stairs, flipping on lights as I go. I open the heavy front door and step away to let her slip in. I can smell the fear on her hair as she passes. It's a kind of iodine smell. I can't describe it, but you know. Or you will know, when you meet it in your own hair someday. Remember I told you that.

She moves, fast, out of the light in the hall and into the dark dining room. From there, her eyes sort of shine out at me. She whispers. "Oh God, Anna. Now they've gotten into my house. They're inside. They were there when I got back. They climbed in the window when I was out. I could hear them up there, just when I put my key into the lock." She's hunched, her little fists curled against her chest. She looks like a rabbit and that's just what she is. And there are lots of foxes in the world, out there in the night. We know that.

So I close the door and lock it and throw all three bolts into place. I can see her shoulders relax with each bolt. I don't speak. I take hold of her arm and sit her down in one of the dining room chairs. I know enough not to light the lamp. And the window shade's already drawn. The dining room is smack in the middle of the house, enclosed. I shut the door to the hall, the door to the pantry, the door to the parlor. I can hear her breathing slow down. I sit down next to her. I can't see her now. It's too dark. But I can smell her and I reach out and take her hand. It's all bones, slick with sweat, slippery as an eel. "OK," I say. "OK. What should we do?"

Her icy fingers circle into my palm. The nails are sharp. "Call

Precinct One," she says. "The cops there know me. I registered with them when I moved in. I always do that, when I move. They know who I am."

Well, I'll just bet they do. Precinct One is right around the corner. And they try, they really do, to keep us safe from murder in our beds. No good against poison though, were they, Mama? Not one damn bit. I clear my throat and tighten my hand around her skinny little claw. "Oh, let's not bother the officers just yet. Why don't you tell me about it first?"

She nods. I can feel her hair brush my shoulder. "It's the ones who kidnapped that SUNY girl, that Melissa Atley. They took her. I know because they took me, too. When I was little. There were posters all over town. $25,000 dollar reward. Remember?"

Remember? Which posters? Which missing girl? There have been lots and lots, haven't there. That Melissa one, she's recent. Her parents were weeping on TV just this spring. But this one? It's a fair bet no one ever offered $25,000 to get this one back, ever. Or 25 cents, either.

"Uh huh." I keep my voice neutral, interested. Not skeptical. It never helps to doubt, when they smell this bad. "How did you get away?"

She laughs. "I been raped, I been cut, I been beat." Little beads of spit hit my cheek with each "b." "I always get away. Always."

"Uh huh. You did, you got away. I mean, here you are."

She loosens her grip on my hand and starts to tap a little beat with one finger. "But they're in my house, right now. They're over there, waiting." Her hand flies out of mine and she stands up. "We have to call Precinct One, Anna. Where's your phone?"

Well, shit. Can't hurt, really. They already know her. So I walk her into the kitchen, where it's just a bit lighter, because the neighbors in back leave a bright outdoor porch light burning, day and night. Who can blame them? It shines over my wild backyard, all full of waving long grasses now, all overgrown with false cucumber and wild grapevines and thistle. My mother and I decided, long ago, that it was best left alone. Lawns and flowers need fertilizer and fertilizer is poison, isn't it? Weeds grow natural, for free. Anyway, the neighbors' light lets her see to dial. She knows the number by heart. She gives her name, first I've heard it. It's Lucy and isn't that a kick. From "light." Lucid. Well, well.

I can tell they don't want to bother with Lucy. She probably calls once a week, easy. She's starting to yell into the phone. I take the receiver from her hand, wipe it on my nightgown, but still feel her spit reaching up to my mouth from the little holes. "Is Sgt. Myers in?" I say. The officer on the other end says, "Who wants him?"

And I start to laugh. "Oh, just say Anna. Say Anna wants him. But first she wants him to send someone to check out this poor child's apartment. Right. Tell him, personally. Yes. Thank you." I hang up, happy to be of service. But it won't really matter in the long run, will it? I mean, they've gotten into her apartment once, she'll never be safe there. The cops will tell her it's fine, no one was ever there, really lady, they weren't there, really. But she knows what she knows. This apartment, like all the others, is contaminated now and she'll move again. Has to.

But for now, little Lucy is looking at me like I'm God. So I sit her down in the kitchen, pour us each a beer and tell her this story, which I've just remembered, this minute. Or maybe it came back the minute her voice called "Anna Rose" into the night and it's taken a bit for me to catch up. Anyway, this is what I tell her: Once, when I was fifteen, I snuck a boy into our attic. There was a little apartment up there, used by displaced persons during the war, my mother said. Distant relatives, on the Jewish side, escaped from Poland. The apartment was pretty dusty and grim by 1964, when I was fifteen, but there was a sturdy cot and just as I wrapped my legs around this particular boy's nice thin hips and pulled him inside, I heard my mother start to yell. "Anna! Oh, my God, Anna." So I disengaged, leaving that boy lying there with his penis hard as a stalk and sticking up into nowhere, drying out in the warm attic air, absolutely ridiculous. And I ran downstairs, wearing not a lot. A garter belt, I think. That's right, we still wore them then, all the time. Pre-panty hose, a moment in history this little Lucy can't imagine. Anyway, I ran down two flights of stairs, metal garters slapping against my thighs all the way. My mother was crouched down on the parlor rug, her arms over her head. Her crutches were flung to each side and she was sobbing. Around and around her head flew a bird. A starling, shiny black and terrified. It landed on lamps and picture frames, door hinges. Things came smashing to the floor. It shat. Its sharp claws tore the curtains. Its wings scattered soot from the chimney it had fallen through, greasy black snow. I wanted to laugh: what a scene. But when I went to shoo it out, opening the front door wide, my mother screamed again. She was staring at me through her clenched hands. "No, Anna, no. Look at you. You're naked. Cover yourself." And then the bird swept over my head, so close I could hear the banging of its panicked wings.

It couldn't quite find the door to freedom and it swooped and swooped around my head. And, just like that, I caught its fear. I started to shriek, a strange high sound I couldn't believe I was making, even as it whistled from my throat. I was absolutely unable to stop screaming. Could not stop. I ducked down. Cowered. Covered my head. And my mother did the bravest thing I've ever seen anyone do, ever. She heaved herself up, uncovering her own head, and she flung herself over me, wrapping her strong arms around my ears, so that I couldn't even hear the bird anymore. She covered my naked back and then all I heard was the pulse of blood through her veins, until the bird was gone and all there was left to do was sweep up the mess and wash the floors and mend the curtains. And block that flue, forever.

Well. Lucy listens to this little fable, politely enough. And she holds her beer in her fists and draws little circles in the dampness the glass makes on the table. But when she leaves, escorted by two nice officers who've searched her apartment and chased the bogeymen away, for tonight, her glass is still full. Not so easily fooled, not her. Not her.

But that's OK. I won't brood just because I haven't been able to make her trust me. And, anyway, Sgt. Joel Myers, whom I've known, for oh, how many years, schoolmate, neighbor, longtime on-and-off-again lover, Joel comes over after his shift and we pour fresh beers and drink them down and we laugh about poor sad Lucy, together. And then he leads me to my bedroom—oh, yes, he knows his way, didn't I just mention a boy in an attic, years and years ago? And this time, I promise you, we don't let his beautiful penis dry out once. Not once.

But when he leaves, he makes me sad. Usually, he doesn't ask, but tonight, I don't know, Lucy maybe, he turns on the porch. The sky is just getting light behind him. He's getting bald and I feel a twinge of worry about that bare spot, right on top of his poor skull, exposed to everything the sky can throw down. He turns around and touches my cheek. "Anna," he says. "Sweet Anna. Are you ever coming out?"

What can I say? My bare toes curl in the doorway. I hold fast. "Go away, Sgt. Myers," I say. My cheek feels tight where his finger rests. "I'll call you when I need you."

He shakes his head. "I won't always come, Anna."

Sure he will. Of course he will. A cop—it's his job to save us. He'll come. I close the door and walk into the kitchen to clean up the beer mugs. Lucy's I pour into the sink. The beer is warm and has no bubbles left. Poor thing. Poor thing.

I go to bed in the growing day and light pushes against my eyelids. Just before I sleep, I feel my body start to beat. I feel my house around me like strong ribs. I pulse, red light throbbing along my eyes. I beat—I am the heart of my house, feeding it with rich, oxygenating blood. It holds me tighter than any lover.

What was that expression my father used to use, long ago, to refer to his money, invested only in the best stocks? Yes—safe as houses, they were. Safe as houses. Exactly.

III. Bats

WELL, IT'S MY OWN fault that the bats come. I do two things wrong—oh, at least two, at least—about three weeks after Joel's visit and Lucy's visitation. Oh, I know why I make mistakes, but knowing doesn't always stop us, does it? I do something dumb because the "For Rent" sign just went up outside Lucy's apartment and I think I'll kind of miss her. And because now it's August and the air has that feel. My mother was scared to death of August, her worst month. Polio month—don't swim, don't go to movies, don't breathe air anyone else has breathed: the world drips poison in August. This fear was not crazy, in 1948, 1949, or in the fifties of my girlhood, trust me. Did I tell you that my mother caught polio when I was a baby? Seemed like a simple cold, like any old virus, at first and then one night, just like that, she couldn't walk and she came crawling to get me out of my crib in the morning, me screaming and soaked and terrified. And her crawling along the hall, calling, "I'm coming, baby, I'm coming." And did I mention that my father went away some years later when it became apparent that her legs would stay all skinny and weak and crooked and she'd have to hump herself around on crutches forever? Well, he did. But he sent money, always, first checks signed by himself, then by lawyers after he was gone. They still come, faithful as ever, those checks. The first one, I was told, came with a note: "My dear, You will never have to go out and work, I promise. I am a coward but I am not cruel. You will stay home with Anna, where you belong." And she did, we did, stayed safe at home. Daddy made it very easy. Still does.

But a person, no matter how careful, still makes mistakes, does things wrong. First mistake: on a hot morning I go up into the attic, for old time's sake. Well, for more, maybe. I've called Joel twice in the past week, at the station as always—we don't bother our lovers at home, do we, through any/all of their marriages—and some polite officer always says he's not available and sticks to it, no matter how many times I say Anna wants

him. Well. I go up to the attic and lie on the dusty cot and look
up into the beams, gazing at the skeleton of my house. But it's
hot enough to roast a turkey up there, so I make my second
mistake. I open the window a crack. Then I crouch down and I
look out the crack into the backyard. There used to be a swing set
out there and a badminton net and croquet wickets. Now there
are twelve-foot nettles and trumpet vines that climb the steel
fence, draping it in veils of green. Masses of dog roses rise like
towers, covered with thorns. Huge blue morning glories bloom
on the roof of the old shed. The yard is pretty in its own wild
way. I get so interested in looking down that I forget to close the
window. Mistakes. Mistakes. I am careless. My mother wouldn't
have forgotten. She kept constant vigil. Oh, and a third. I've let
bats into my head, haven't I, watching little Lucy come and go
into the night? And I've remembered that black bird, shitting
fear into the parlor. That's enough. Sometimes, all you have to
do is think about something and that's as bad as inviting it over
for tea. Think it and it comes. Invoke. Summon. Conjure. My
mother burned my Ouija board, years and years ago, for good
reason. For now I've gone and called up bats.

You can guess the rest. That night I am sound asleep. The
humid air is spinning through the fans in my room and so I
am almost deaf to the small noises of the night. But not quite.
A thud, a soft odd whir. A noise not of this house, it wakes me
from happy dreams. I am groggy when I walk into the hall, or
I wouldn't do it. I would stay in my room until morning, stuff
blankets into the cracks around the door. I would huddle under
my sheets, I would put my pillows over my ears. It is another
mistake but I am sleepy and I do it. I step into the hall and the
bats are upon me. They fill the air with their odor, their leathery

upside-down smell, their perversely furry flying bodies. Winged rats. I begin to scream. It is a sound I have hoped never to hear, ever again, but it comes out of my mouth in sheets. I stand in my hall, in my house, and I scream and scream and scream. I tumble and claw my way down the stairs to the front door. I throw all the bolts and open it wide—but I cannot push myself out. The bats fill the house with their horrible squeaking but I cannot, cannot go out into the huge empty night. So I lie on my doorstep and I cry, a great big baby, a-stink with fear, filling the air with iodine and slobber. Inside my blubbering, oddly enough, I still know things. I know that Joel won't come and my mother will not cover my back. My spine sticks up into the night air and I can't stop crying.

I'm so awash in my own stupid noise, it turns out, that I don't even hear little Lucy come to save me. I don't hear her until she is standing above me in the hall, giggling. It is a sound so foreign to Lucy's throat that I look up. She is fully dressed and she has her hands on her hips. "For Christ's sake, Anna," she says. "They're only bats. They can't hurt you."

Well. This is what she does to get rid of them. She walks into my house, where they whir and swoop and spin, and she goes into every room and she flips every switch until the house blazes with light. She opens every window, wide, and throws up the screens. Then she comes back and sits with me in the hall. "They'll leave," she says. "Bats hate light." She takes my head into her lap and she hums a little. I push my face into her blue-jeaned thigh and I smell nothing but clean cotton.

When the house gets perfectly quiet and we're pretty sure the bats are gone, I sit up. I wait awhile and then I stand up. I walk into my kitchen and I reach to the highest shelf and I take down Mama's last bottle of gin. I pour two big glasses and I hand one to Lucy. "Drink it," I say. "It won't hurt you."

But she can't. She just spins the glass in her fingers and smiles like an angel. "Walk me home?" she says.

But I can't. All I can do is take one step beyond the jambs and that damn near kills me. But I owe her something, don't I? So I stand on my porch and watch her go, holding off the gangs, the pit bulls, the fat janitor, the rapists, the kidnappers, the murderers, the whole stinking filthy poisonous world, fiercely, with my eyes alone. When she reaches her door, before she climbs the stairs to her haunted house, all alone, she turns and gives a jaunty little wave, the second bravest thing I've ever seen.

The Trojan Cat:

A Drama in Three Acts

I

THE FIRST DEAD mouse could have been an accident. You thought so; anyone would have thought so. Innocent mouse, dead on the deck: tiny and softly gray, white-tummied, no obvious sign of blood. You pick it up by its tail and throw it into the yard of the disgusting man across the street.

The pile of three mice is more suspicious. No, on closer inspection, there are two mice and something related but not quite, a vole? Whatever: three rodents do not simply decide to die together—all for one, one for all!—in a neat little pyramidal heap on your front deck. And you can't just swing them by their little stiff tails, sailing them off across the street. For two reasons: Walt, the horrible old man, is home, out mowing his grass for the fourth time in one afternoon, never mind that it is mid-October and the grass is no longer growing. Walt is a drunk, a total nutcase, and you don't want to draw his attention. Second, the not-quite-a-mouse has no tail, only a tiny stumpy thing you refuse to touch. So, this is work that requires a shovel. When you go to the garage to get the shovel, you meet the likely sculptor of dead-rodent cairns: a dark-striped, ragged, lynx-eared cat whose head is far too big for his scrawny body. He stares at you imperiously. You are expected, you know, to express gratitude. The mice he might have eaten have, instead, come to you in some sort of sacred kitty-ritual of gifting.

You lean on the shovel and gaze into the cat's yellow eyes. You have resisted, all these years. You have vowed not to become a pathetic old woman with a hundred cats. You read the papers; you watch the news. Just last month it was two sisters up in Albany: Eighty cats taken from their two cars. Forty more from their house. You watched, hand over your mouth in horror, as one of the sisters—presumably the saner of the two, despite her wild white hair and twitching eye—explained that they love their cats, that they feed them, that they do their best. They do their goddamn *best*. You watch her fall apart, as the camera and reporters back away. She reaches out to them with empty, withered arms.

You live alone and you rarely speak to neighbors and you are, you know, the perfect candidate for this exact kind of craziness. But not quite: inside your tiny house sits your savior, your old dog, Alex. He is blind and he is deaf and he limps. And he will not, would not tolerate cats in his house. End of discussion. He's been with you for fifteen years.

You bend and rub a line down the head and back of the striped cat, smoothing back his rough fur, feeling the healed scars that pock his skin. "Phooey on you, buddy," you tell him. "Can't catch me."

You go inside and feed the dog, who still enjoys his chow. As do you.

LEAVES FALL AND days darken, and the striped cat leaves nightly offerings. Chipmunk, mouse, sparrow, bat. You can't help but chuckle. You buy three cans of cat food, generic store brand, and feed him on the deck. You name him, in what you consider a fit of brilliance, Oscar Wilde. Long ago, you read books by the dozens, before your eyes grew dim.

II

WHEN THE FIRST real snow blows in, late in November, it covers the deck—and the latest tiny corpse—with white. You sit in your chair, looking out into the storm. On your lap, you hold Alex. Well, what remains. A coffee can of Alex's ashes. He was, you know, the last dog you will own. To rescue another from the shelter, well, even that would be unfair at this stage of the game. Dogs mourn, too.

The houses trembles with winter—the wind outside, the rattle of the old furnace. You keep it set very low; the house never heats to more than 56 degrees. Oil is expensive and the house is full of drafts. The tin can—are cans still made of tin?—feels like ice in your hands.

That night, when the storm has piled drifts around the foundation of your house, Oscar comes to the window, yellow eyes circled in frost, whiskers stiff with rime. He is standing in the snow-packed window box, his mouth open in a silent mew.

You open the door. Bring him in. He settles, after rubbing his cheeks on every surface in the house, on the one heating vent in the living room. He curls there, soaking up all the warmth.

The room grows even colder. When you pick him up and bring him into your lap, it is like holding onto heat itself. Your aching fingers grow supple when you plunge them deep inside his fur. Inside there, your hands feel young.

By December, you have two more cats. One, a small mist-colored female, you call Miss Kitty. The other, a brilliant orange, is Snazzle. The house comes alive with their running and leaping and pouncing. You laugh, quite often now. You smile at the man across the street, who may be just as lonely as yourself. As you used to be. You wave at him, speak a jaunty hello. There is, now, a place in your heart for pity.

February. There are the smallest signs of spring, just beyond the deck. (No more mouse-offerings are left. They have done their work.) The tiniest, the earliest of the crocuses you planted forty falls ago, are up, the yellow and the white, fragile as dragonfly wings. The big sturdy purples come later; you're looking forward to that.

You open the front window, just a bit. You sniff the fresh air, damp and silky. It reminds you that the air inside your house is ripe with cat. The cardboard boxes you line with shredded newspapers, for litter—three such boxes at last count—tend to overflow. They grow soggy on the bottoms, sometimes, when you forget to empty them. The cat food in the six bowls sometimes hardens and remains there, a dark crust. But the house is so alive! Mr. Kitten and Bear and Moose and Max and Mousie and Honey and Bill and Lupine and Sadie and The Bambino—the biggest, bounciest, funniest cat of all—are so full of energy. Sometimes Oscar, the patriarch, hisses at them all and slides under the bed in a fit of pique. But you can always jolly him out with a special treat or a long rub. He is, you whisper in his ear, your favorite still. You're kept awake nights by the flea bites on your ankles and the hissing of the occasional fight. You lie in the dark, scratch and listen. This watchful sleeplessness seems familiar—it is almost like having babies in the house again. No, not babies. Teenagers. Yes, quarreling, troublesome, late-night teenagers, back from dark doings of their own, sending waves of beer and sweat up and down the hall. You always liked those frantic, noisy nights. As you like these.

Honey and Mousie and Miss Kitty and Snazzle are growing wide and broody; things are afoot.

III

SNAZ IS THE FIRST to give birth, on the end of your bed, early March. You sit up all night with her—not touching, just watching. She needs no help; she has done all this before. By dawn, there are five damp blind kittens mewling and pushing at Snazzle's teats. Her eyes are closed, her labor over. You lean over the little nest she has kneaded in the covers. You breathe, deep, deep. The smell is indescribable—it catches in your throat, brings tears to your eyes. It is salt, it is blood, it is birth. It is life, at last, come into your house, once again. In your dry breasts, you feel again the tingling, the imminent flow of your milk, letting down. You are perfectly sane; you know there is no milk. But you feel it, all the same.

You settle down to name the kittens, all beautiful five, according to their colors and your memories, from so far back they are like dreams, of growing up on the farm: Straw, Alfalfa, Timothy, Milky—one of the kittens a miraculous white!—and

Cornsilk. Always, always there were nests of kittens in the hayloft; always the chance, at least, that your mother would let you bring one home. You chose very carefully, the one you would love and save.

THE FIRST WEEK of March, there is a late blizzard, snowdrifts sculpted into white waves. Inside, there are twenty-odd kittens and two more adults. You don't remember where they all came from, cannot recall letting all of them in. You can't keep up with the naming. You sometimes step in piles of cat shit, heaped in unexpected places. You run out of cat food and when the snow subsides you walk to Stewarts for more. You see how people at the counter wrinkle their noses when you pay. You sniff at yourself on the walk home, cans bumping against your leg in their plastic bags. If you stink of cat piss, you can't smell it.

Two days later, you find three dead kittens in a closet, all gray, all stiff and cold, eyes sealed shut, pink tongues protruding. You don't know who they belong to but you mourn them anyway. You hold each tiny body tenderly in your palm before tucking it away in the garbage.

ONCE OR TWICE the phone rings and its particular ring sounds official, sounds like someone barging in. You don't answer.

A few peaceful days go by. The last of the hard-crusted snow swirls away in rain showers. The purple crocuses have come up and begun to unfurl, lovely. There is sunshine, a hint of warmth. Maybe things will remain as they are, if you stay very still and very watchful. You tuck your face into Oscar's neck and breathe his wild-tame smell. Snazzle pats you with a gentle paw.

One day, a woman with a clipboard comes to the front door and you don't answer that, either. Backed against a wall, peeking out the window, you see her talking to the man across the street and he is waving his arms, pointing up into the branches of the big maple in your front yard. The branches are still bare but beginning to redden, sap rising. Among them, you imagine that you can see a multitude of tails, curling down from the branches, streamers of multicolored fur. Festive. Utterly beautiful.

You wait. The house is full of warmth and energy. The kittens romp and play, batting and running and climbing. The elders sleep in squares of sunlight, their perfect paws twitching gently. The cats are dreaming elegant dreams. It is a house of joy. How will you explain that, to people with clipboards? How can they understand this glorious gift that's come to you, so late in life? So unexpected, so precious?

How will you survive, when they take it all away?

You hold Oscar on your lap. Will they leave you one? Please, please. Will they leave Oscar to purr and knead on your lap? Please God, let them leave just one.

You hear the knock again. Louder, pounding. Voices, calling. Demanding to be let in. You know they will not go away, will never leave you in peace. You look at the calendar you've tacked to the wall. You will remember this date.

You have to laugh. The Ides. It is the Ides. You lean into the warmth of fur and whisper, *"Et tu, Brute?"*

Oscar leaps from your lap, heading for the door.

Praise Be to an Afflicting God

EITHER THE WATER WAS RISING or the houses were sinking. Probably both. The way luck usually ran on Incubator Lane in Van Luykensville, New York, both: rising underground lake and falling houses. Troubles, here, came in torrents; triumphs only trickled.

"Praise be to an afflicting God." Peter Johnson had been perusing the Puritans again. Attorney-at-law when he felt like it and heavy-drinking book-reader when he didn't, Peter picked books that were appropriate to the times, he always said. Imminent disaster called for Puritans: hellfire essays, brimstone sermons, and bedeviled prayers. "It's over, our little time on this little street in this little town. Live with it, bro." Peter pulled his flannel shirt sleeves down over his fingers. It was June, but only 52 degrees. It had been raining for a month and a half. Peter's boots were sunk to the ankles in the muddy lawn behind his house.

Aaron Ooms's sneakers were sunk only to the laces. Aaron would, of course, sink down at a slower rate, since he was a whole lot lighter than Peter. Almost everyone was. He looked across his fence and said, "God, shit. It's the developers. They cut down the orchards. Apple trees drink, what, fifty gallons of water a day? The fuckers cut down hundreds of trees. So they could put up fourteen McMansions. What a deal." He leaned against the old maple tree that created a bulge in the fence. The tree, rooted there a hundred-and-some years ago, felt oddly loose, as if its roots were giving up their grip on the land. Below, in the deep gully that lay beyond the yards, the rail tracks rusted. The tips of fifteen granite gravestones shone silver in the rain.

Peter shrugged. Drops of rain pearled on his bald head, then danced off down the rolls of his neck, vanishing into folds of flesh. "Praise be to afflicting developers, then. Comes to the same thing. Our houses are disappearing into the primordial ooze. Theirs are putting in heated swimming pools. Jacuzzis. Got to be evolution, right? We're dinosaurs; they're mammals. Our time has passed. Sayonara, suckers."

At least three-fifths of the time, Aaron didn't know what the hell Peter was talking about. He suspected that at least two-fifths of the time, neither did Peter. He squinted his good eye and looked back at his house. It wasn't so much *lower* as it was just a bit off kilter. If you took a T square and put it up against any one of the walls, he bet you'd see that something funny was going on in the foundation. He felt his heart contract. He'd lived in that little two-bedroom ranch house since he was ten years old—thirty-four fucking years now. His mother had bought the place with the old man's life insurance money in 1972. When these little houses went for, what, about five thousand bucks?

Himself, he had no insurance: not medical, not life, not fire. Not flood. And, as far as he knew, neither did anyone else who lived on the street. They weren't insurance kind of people. They were the kind of people who lived in certain expectation of disaster but didn't—or couldn't—prepare for it. Aaron pulled his sweatshirt hood tighter over his head. "I think the rain's slowing down," he said. "The sky's lighter."

Peter looked at him, a kind of amused sadness in his face. "Right. And lightning never strikes twice, does it, bro?"

"Fuck you." Aaron turned on his heel—his good heel—and tried to walk away, fast. But his sneakers squelched and the whole effect was pretty pathetic. Still, he tried to keep his dignity. Always had. It never worked, but he always tried.

"*It is good for me that I have been afflicted.* That's Psalm 119, David speaking." Peter laughed. "*Affliction I wanted, and affliction I had, full measure.* That's Mary Rowlandson, in 1676, after being captured by the Indians and having most of her family slaughtered. Her six-year-old daughter, taken with her, died on the ninth day of their captivity, in her arms. *C'est la vie, ma amie.*" He pulled his heavy, mud-clumped boots out of the ground and walked, head down, toward his own back porch.

JANICE VAN ALLEN tucked the afghan around her mother's shoulders and looked out the window. She pulled a strand of her frizzing brown-gray hair behind her ear.

Her mother gave a little jump in her wheelchair. "We're going," she shouted. "I feel it."

Janice didn't even turn. Her mother had been doing this for days, saying that she felt the ground giving out underneath her wheels, shouting out that they were falling. "No, we're not," Janice said. She held the net curtain aside; it smelled musty. Everything did. The sheets on her bed, the clothes in her closet. Her own body, she thought. Well, shit, things not in use got mildewed, didn't they? And her body hadn't been used in a while. Peter used to use it—and very nicely, too—before he got so heavy. Now, it was one of his more bizarre gentlemanly notions, that he shouldn't put his weight on anyone else's bones. Not even if her bones were aching to be held down. Crushed even. Something. Anything. She remembered that she'd once fondled Peter's penis, telling him how appropriate it was that both of his names—first and sur—were slang words for that very organ. He'd agreed, not one bit humble.

Mrs. Van Allen laughed. "You might think that, my girl. But I can feel it. Right through the wheels of this thing." She smacked a palm on the arm of her chair. "Metal conducts vibrations. I can feel things you can't."

Janice turned. "Like a groundhog?" She smiled, to take any potential insult out of her words. "Prairie dog? Mole? You predict earthquakes, too, old lady?"

Her mother's lips pursed. "I believe I might. If one was coming." Then she tilted her head on her thin neck. The afghan was already slipping and the crumpled skin on her throat showed white, with blue rivers of veins running through it. "Well, the hell with it. Do we have any bologna for lunch?"

"No," Janice said. She turned and took hold of the handles on the wheelchair.

"Damn. What, then?" Her mother's head tilted back, now, her eyes rolling up to find Janice's face. The eyes were deep brown, still, with the little golden flecks that Janice had inherited.

Janice leaned down and put her lips on her mother's forehead. Everyone who knew the Van Allens thought that Janice had sacrificed her own life to care for her mother. What everyone didn't know was that her mother was the only person that Janice had ever truly loved. Not the only person she'd ever wanted, but the only one loved. The seventh Van Allen child, Janice had waited impatiently for her brothers and sisters to leave home, to have her mother—and her bedroom—all to herself. "We have liverwurst," she said.

Mrs. Van Allen smiled. "Well, that's all right, then."

IT WASN'T REALLY Incubator Lane, of course. It had an official name that no one but the post office used. Incubator Lane was just a snotty sobriquet—Peter's word, that Aaron had looked up and decided he liked—given to the street by the people who had lived, after the War, in the big, four-bedroom colonials that lined the real streets in Van Luykensville. This little street, with its five shotgun houses, had been especially created in 1947 for the workers on the rail line that ran through the village, right behind the Lane, just below the sharp slope that backed the yards. The guys who'd come home from the War, put away their weapons and picked up track-repair tools, along with young wives. One of those young wives was Mrs. Van Allen, nineteen years old and wonderfully fertile: she'd produced seven children, lickety-split. And, indeed, the houses came to be called incubators because of their boxy shape and, it was implied, the fact that the trashy people in them bred like bunnies. In the early years, the 1950s, babies had bloomed like a cash crop, filling the yards. In the 1960s, hippies moved in, planted gardens, and the rail line shut down. From that time forward, the tracks ran rusty and empty, wild flowers and weeds filling in for boxcars and tankers. But the houses remained.

In 1972, Aaron and his mother moved in—Aaron dazzled in one eye and crippled on one side from the ball of electricity that had rolled down through the center of his father's barn on June 13, 1971. Aaron and his dad had both been walking along the row, clanking the stanchions shut around the cows' necks when that lightning ball came rolling, turning the air blue. They'd both stopped to stare—it was like nothing they'd ever seen. Like a space ship. Like some kind of magic trick. Like hellfire. Then that ball of light took a fast left turn, bouncing into the metal stanchions that held the whole herd: fifty Holsteins and six pretty little Jersey cows that they kept just for the cream. The cows went down like black-and-white dominoes. Aaron's father went down with them. Aaron felt only a gentle tingling up his side, a running of warm fingers against his skin, at first. Then a screeching in his ears and a green-out of his vision. He thought he smelled something burning, but then the rain came and there was only the smell of sweet wet grass—the hay they'd cut that very afternoon, just before the unexpected, unpredicted, unusual line of storms rolled in.

In the midst of all the mourning for his father, only Aaron, from his Shriners Hospital bed, seemed to remember and feel the loss of the cows: their soft brown eyes, long lashed. Their flicking tails and expressive ears. He looked it up later in his World Books: cows are fifty times more sensitive to electricity than people are. And they'd been fastened in, enclosed in metal neck bars: they'd been sitting ducks. He'd told Peter about it—they were both ten years old, then—and Peter had gone ahead and looked up ball lightning, too, in his Encyclopedia Britannica. Ball lightning was, he'd reported, a rare phenomenon that no one really understood. It often preceded the actual storm; there was no way, really, to prepare for it or to prevent it. It was, Peter had said—even then, Peter said things like this—a pure act of

God. God said, *Slam bam, thank you, m'am.* And then God said, according to Peter, *AMF YO YO.* Of course, Aaron had to ask him what that meant and Peter, giggling, had explained that it was a note that doctors—Peter's father was a doctor, himself, so he knew—left in the charts of particularly hopeless patients when they went home for the night, a note addressed to some hapless intern: *Adios, Mother Fucker: You're On Your Own.* At the sound of the mf-word, both boys had sucked in their cheeks, rolled their eyes, and laughed like wild loons. In 2006, no one understood ball lightning—or its aftereffects—a whole lot better and Aaron had given up on understanding anything, much, anyway.

And only three of the houses on his street were still inhabited; the other two—numbers 2 and 4—were blown away in 2000, in the only tornado ever to hit this part of New York state, on the only street that had suffered a direct hit in the whole blooming state. Now there were only numbers 3 and 5 on the left, just above the slope and the tracks, and 6 on the right side of the road. Old Mrs. Van Allen and her still-pretty daughter, Janice, now middle aged herself and no longer quite so wild as she'd been in her youth, lived in 6. Peter inhabited 5—Peter had moved in in 1996, after losing his own four-bedroom colonial to one of his former wives. Aaron, who'd never had even one wife, in 3. As it looked, they would be the last, ever, to call Incubator Lane home.

AARON WAS IN his basement, watching rivulets run down the walls. The sump pump was running, nonstop, but nothing could really keep up with waters rising from the earth and falling from the sky, both. And there was someone banging on his front door.

"I'm coming," he yelled. "Hold on." The basement steps were

jerry rigged, like everything else in the house. On the bottom half, the steps were just loose boards balanced on concrete blocks that were themselves balanced, not perfectly, on each other. And, in the best of times, it took Aaron a while to get up any set of stairs: he had to put his right leg up, then use his right hand to grab the denim of his jeans on the left leg, and haul that leg up. Balance. Rest. Breathe. And again: right leg up, et cetera. A marathon of effort. And whoever was at the door wasn't patient, banging away like a jack hammer. And not likely local, either, since no one local would use a front door on Incubator Lane—the front doors were warped affairs that opened directly into the living rooms, bringing dirt and whatnot straight into the house. The kitchen doors, on the sides of the houses, were the real doors, where three generations of housewives kept mud mats ready. "Hold the fuck on," Aaron yelled.

He flung the door open and tried to gauge the relative assholery of the person banging on it. He'd spent the past thirty-five years doing this—if you're crippled and poor and half-blind, you meet more than your share of assholes. Or, as Peter said, normal people simply become assholes in your presence, *ipso facto*. Either way, the world was full of them.

As always, the man's face first appeared as a flashing green circle of light rimmed with rainbows—the vision of his left eye taking over. When he was able to focus with his right eye and bring the face into some kind of relative clarity, Aaron saw that it was a bland, official sort of face above a suit and tie. A damp suit, emitting wet-dog odor. He held the door open and stepped back. "Come in out of the rain," he said.

The man stepped inside and his face showed the shock that people pretty much always registered upon first seeing Aaron—

the initial widening of eyes, then the quick shrinking of pupils, as if the eyes themselves didn't want to let Aaron's appearance in: the head singed bald on the left, the useless arm dangling, the permanent half-smirk on the left side of the face. But, to his credit, this guy recovered pretty quickly and cleared his throat. "Sorry to bother you," he said. He pulled a clipboard out from under one arm. "I'm from the State." He flashed some kind of ID card under Aaron's gaze, but it was all a green blur.

"Good. You here to help us fill out disaster forms?" Aaron asked. "So we can get emergency loans? Or, something? Shore up the houses, maybe?"

Peter's voice came through the open doorway, "Oh, certainly. And then they'll send the Army Corps of Engineers to build us some really great levees, too. Just like New Orleans. Next will arrive the Cavalry. Then Rin Tin Tin, to the rescue. Yo, Rinny." Peter stomped up onto the porch and stepped into the living room. He held out an enormous hand. "Hello, I live next door. I'm Mr. Ooms's attorney. May I be of assistance?"

The man from the State turned and shook Peter's hand. It was obvious that he was glad to have a non-cripple—even if the man was hugely fat and breathing hard, just from the walk across the driveway—to speak to. "Thank you," he said. "I've been sent to assess the state of the state-owned graveyard." He waved a hand in the air. "I understand that it's somewhere behind these houses."

Aaron backed up and let Peter take over—he would anyway. He leaned against his mother's hutch and waited.

Peter scowled. "The slave graveyard, you mean?"

The man checked his clipboard. "Yes. Where the remains of the Van Luykens' servants are buried. Mid-18th through mid-19th century, I understand. It's a state historical site."

"Slaves, man." Peter put a finger on the clipboard. "Not servants. Servants can leave. Slaves can't. There's a difference. People in New York State—the Empire State, remember—don't like to admit it, but we had slaves. Up until the mid-1800s. 1827, officially, but some of the patroons, well, they held on to their property a whole lot longer. We *owned* people. Right here in River City. Us." He punched the finger in the direction of the man's chest.

Aaron had to smile. Now this poor state guy had gone and done it. Touched one of Peter's many sore spots. Peter always claimed to be one-eighth black and one-sixteenth Indian, although there wasn't a sign of that ancestry in his skin or eyes or hair—when he'd had hair, it was blond and straight, always flopping in his eyes. But he took this purported ancestry seriously and allied himself with oppressed races everywhere.

The man backed up and cleared his throat. "Well, yes, sir. It does say 'slaves.' You're correct. The remains of approximately fifteen slaves were interred. . . ."

"Approximately? Approximately?" Peter held up one big hand and began counting off, on his fingers. "Isabel Legget, Philip Collins, Harriet Burget—those are the adults. The rest were only kids when they went into the care of the Lord: Charles Van Volkenburg, aged one year, three months, and five days. Francis DeFreest. William G., Harriet A., Sylvestes—although you have to wonder if that's not a misspelling for 'Sylvester,' an error forever graven into stone. Rachel M. Two with illegible names: one the son of Tobias and Betty Toby, one that just says 'Children of Peter and Harriet Burget'. Four that are just broken stones: no names anymore. Deaths range from 1820 to 1860. Lots of the kids died in the summer of 1860. I surmise some sort of fever came and. . . ."

"Well, I don't know about any of that. I don't have individual names."

Peter's face darkened. "But they did, mister. They had names. Dutch surnames, given by their goddamn *masters*. But real, individual names. And they loved their dead babies. Do you know what little Charles Van Volkenburg's stone reads? It starts *Sleep sweet babe*. . . ."

Aaron had heard all of this before, many times. And he'd read the stones, too, until he'd come to be ashamed of his own Dutch name. He leaned forward. "Excuse me. I don't much care who they are—were. But I want to get this straight. Do you mean that the state of New York is going to help dead people but not us? Our houses are about to be buried in some kind of sinkhole, mudslide, whatever, and you're here to tend to the fucking dead?"

The man's mouth tightened. "I don't know. I'm only here to assess the graves." He ran a hand across his head, messing up his fringe of reddish hair. "Look, you guys. I'm just a lowly state worker, okay? That's all I am. I'm a peon. Don't blame me."

Suddenly, Peter laughed and slapped the man on the back. "Ah, a brother under the skin. Come with me, fellow lackey. I'll introduce you to our most quiet neighbors. Aaron, I bet if you look, you can find us three beers in that Frigidaire of yours."

THE SLAVE GRAVES, as everyone in Van Luykensville called them, lay just between the railroad tracks and the backyards of Incubator Lane. In a grassy knoll, fenced in with black wrought iron. The graves were cared for by village workers, the same two guys who mowed the ball field and put up Christmas lights in the village square. Todd and Sam: not the brightest of duos, but they respected the dead and were meticulous about cutting the grass around the graves and trying to keep village kids from spray-painting the headstones. And/or screwing right on top of somebody's body on summer nights—Aaron had heard them down there, sometimes, the girls squealing and the boys laughing. He was envious as all hell, listening to them, horny and alone and pissed off about being horny and alone and having to listen. So he always said someone should put a stop to it. But Peter always said to let them go at it—it wouldn't last long, in any case. He said that the blood of youth ran fast and their semen even faster. And, he said that he didn't think his ancestors, lying in that cold black dirt, would mind a little twist and shout going on above their heads. He said that he was sure that his ancestors had twisted and shouted a bit in their time. Probably not, Aaron thought. They were slaves, man, he'd replied once; they couldn't breathe, never mind shout, unless their owners let them. Peter had frowned and said, "They were people, first; slaves, second."

IT WAS HARD for Aaron to get down the slope and carrying three beers in a canvas sack slung over his shoulder wasn't making it any easier. Peter and the state guy just slipped and slid their way down the grassy hill. Aaron had to walk to the end of the block—step with the right leg, swing the left forward, et cetera—to the woods and then go down the set of crude steps that he and Peter had constructed as kids. The steps were made of logs laid crossways, dirt packed between them. They were muddy now and Aaron saw that a lot of the dirt was washing away, leaving big gaps under the logs, gaps through which water ran in mini-falls. Shit.

By the time Aaron got to the graves, the state guy was crouching down, his hand on Isabel Legget's grave—the matriarch, dead at seventy-seven years of age. He was trying to write on his clipboard, but the paper was so damp and slippery that the ink from his pen wouldn't take. He sighed and stood up. He ran his hand through his hair again, making little muddy streaks. He looked so pathetic that Aaron handed him his beer first. Then he popped his can open, and tossed one to Peter. The state guy said, "Hey, thanks, but I'm not allowed. . . ."

"Pish tosh. Fire, locusts and floods. It's been pouring for forty days and forty nights. And we're real short on arks. Drink your frigging beer." Peter tilted his can back and poured the beer straight down his throat.

The guy shrugged and took a gulp.

A voice from the top of the slope called to them. "Hey, are girls invited to this party?"

Aaron looked up and waved at Janice Van Allen. "Come on down." He watched as she made her way down. She slipped once, landing on her butt. He saw that she was barefoot, holding a pair of sandals in one hand. When she reached the bottom and came toward them, he held out his can of beer. "Only took one sip," he said. "Want it?"

Her white pants were muddy around the butt and she was brushing her hand over her backside. Her shirt was wet. It pulled over her chest and he could see the lines where her bra bit into her breasts. His belly tightened. Janice was still pretty enough to do that to him. He knew that, for a while, she'd been Peter's girl—somewhere between the first wife and the second—or maybe even during the first wife, Peter wouldn't ever say, he was such a gentleman. About some things. But he hadn't seen Peter's bulky shadow slipping into or out of her house for a long, long while. So maybe it was his time—maybe even a crippled half-blind man got a shot, somewhere along the line of a single woman's aging. Janice, in her youth, had carried on her affairs right across the street from Aaron's house. None too discreetly. He'd lusted for Janice for thirty years: for the girl, the young woman, the mature woman. To no avail. So far.

"No, thanks." Janice slapped her palms together, trying to get rid of the mud, but then gave up. "I just wanted to know what you guys were up to." She looked at Peter, watching the remainder of his beer go down his throat in one long swallow. "Hello to you, too, Mr. Johnson," she said. Fat bastard: he wanted beer more than he wanted sex—or even affection (she'd never, ever said love, wouldn't have even tried to trick him with that one), these days. And he looked like he'd put on another fifty pounds. Fatter bastard.

Peter nodded to her. "Ms. Van Allen. Another lovely day in upstate New York, is it not?" He pointed his beer can toward the state guy, who also nodded, but kept drinking his beer. "This is—well, I don't know his name—a representative of our sovereign government, here in the year of our Lord two ought ought six. He's here to rescue these old bones from the coming deluge." He pointed at the graves.

"Well, I'm not so sure. I've got to write up a report and send it out. . . ." The guy shook his head. "Slowly, slowly. You know, that's how the wheels turn and all. I'm going to try, but, hey." He finished the beer and handed the empty can to Aaron. "Thanks, you guys. I'll do what I can."

Aaron gripped the cold can. "Can you, at least, tell somebody that there are real live people here, right here, right now, that might need rescuing, too? I mean, our homes." He could feel anger slip into his left eye and the world put on a luminous green overcoat. This always happened when he got upset—his right eye gave up and his left took over. And the world turned strange, as if someone was spraying Day-Glo paint into the air. He could see the state guy heading up the slope, his feet sliding out from under him. His back turned. "Hey, asshole," he shouted. "I mean it. We're fucking *alive* here and those are our fucking *homes* up there. You better *do* something, man. Someone had better fucking well *do* something. I mean it."

Janice put her hand on his arm. "Hush, Aaron," she said. "Don't."

He saw her, through a veil, greenly. But her eyes flickered with those little gold speckles and her hair curled wild around her face. He shook his head, clearing the green mist from his vision. In his hand, the beer can was crushed. Its edges were sharp and his palm was bleeding.

Janice's eyes looked teary. She rubbed them. "Hey," she said. "Come on up. Mom and I are having lunch in a minute. We've got liverwurst. There's plenty. You, too, Counselor," she said, in Peter's direction.

Peter was standing with his head down, staring at the grave below his feet: Philip Collins, who died in 1849, at the age of sixty-seven. He tried to picture the man, as he might have looked in his youth. Truly black African skin, shiny. Muscled, strong. White teeth shining out, on the rare occasions that Philip smiled. Peter bent and touched the cold wet stone that marked Phillip's last, and probably best, bed. "*God sees good to cast some men into the furnace of affliction and then beats them at His anvil into what frame he pleases,*" he said. "That's Anne Bradstreet, bro, 1867. A white lady poet. You never met her."

"Oh, please." Janice rolled her eyes. She hooked her arm into Aaron's and they started to walk toward the woods and the steps.

AFTER LUNCH, THE SUN came out. Peter had never showed up at Janice's house, so it had been just Aaron, Janice and Mrs. Van Allen. They'd had thick sandwiches, with lettuce and tomato and lots of mayo—Aaron himself never bothered to buy all that stuff, so it was a treat—and lemonade and chips. And, afterward, real chocolate cupcakes that Janice had baked that very morning. She'd smiled at him. "No reason not to cook, just because the end is near, right?" She'd touched his shoulder with her fingertips. "In this the year 2006, *anno domini,* as Peter would say. Pompous ass."

And that made Aaron feel so brave that he'd said that he wanted to take a look at the old farm, while the sun was shining. He'd been meaning to, all month, he said. And did she want to come along? While he waited for her reply, his heart climbed into his throat and lodged there.

She tilted her head toward her mother.

The old lady winked at her. "I'll be going in for my nap, anyway, and you've got hours before you've got to get to work. Go on, children. Have fun."

Janice stood up and gathered the plates and glasses. "Okay," she said. "Might as well make hay while the sun shines, right?" And then she actually blushed.

Aaron's heart moved down from his throat. It began to beat again, in his chest. Then it kept on moving down and started to beat in his groin.

PETER WATCHED THE SUN light up the whiskey in his glass—the liquid went from plain brown to glowing amber. He watched as Janice Van Allen's Volkswagen bug pulled from her driveway, Aaron in the passenger seat. He raised his glass to them: *"L'chaim, my friends. To life."* He tilted the whiskey into his throat.

Peter's clothes were still damp and muddy. He made his way down the long skinny hall—an addition to the original cottage—to his bedroom in the back. He touched the walls all along the hallway. He wasn't really that attached to the house; he'd lived here for ten years, not for thirty, like Aaron. But, still. He sat down on his bed, feeling the springs sink beneath his weight. He pulled off his thick gray socks and looked down at his bluish wrinkled feet. He wrestled off his sodden sweatpants. Then he gave up on getting re-dressed. He reached into the top drawer of his dresser and pulled out the photo: the very first Mrs. Johnson. Chantal. No one—not even Aaron—knew that he'd been married three times, not twice. Chantal—a four-month marriage, back when he was in Boston, in law school. Chantal. He studied the face: deep brown skin; warm, open smile; shining black eyes. Hair all braided up. Hands on hips. Chantal, who'd walked out of their tiny little apartment one sunny day and never come back. Who'd looked him straight in the eye and said good-bye without a tear. Who'd said, and yes, he could quote: *You're not a drunk yet, but you will be. I'm not about to wait around to see it happen. There's something missing in you. There's some kind of hole in your soul. You try to fill it up with other people's words. Other people's skin color. But you can't. Beer can't fill it either. It's a damn shame, but that's the way it is.* That's what she's said. And she was perfectly correct in saying so. The hole gaped wider every day: books, drink, friends. Nothing filled it. All the food in the world didn't make a dent. There was no reason for it. It just was.

He put the photo back in the drawer. He settled back against the pillows. Janice and Aaron. After all these years. Well, why not? Why the hell not? He laughed: *The Wine of astonishment.* That was Mary Rowlandson again, back from captivity, lone survivor, astonished by life. Who was he, to question?

AARON'S FATHER'S FARM LAND lay shining in the sunlight. He and Janice sat on the top of the hill, looking down at it. Where the alfalfa and corn had grown, there were now seven completed houses. Where the apple orchard used to blossom, every May, three completed and four half-completed foundations. Where the pond had served up bass, an artificial lake, adorned with fountains. Each house boasted a yard of two to three acres. Every one had a special feature. A turret. Fake Tudor beams. White clapboards that were really vinyl, a slate roof that was really just shingle, a stone front that was really plastic. Or some other damn thing, fakery all. Every one had a huge air-conditioning unit somewhere on the property, big green metal boxes that they'd tried to hide behind bushes or fake gray boulders. Behind them all, off in the west, the Catskill Mountains, blue in the distant sky. The silhouette of the mountains was the same as it had always been. The exact same configuration Aaron's dad had pointed out to him, always there at the western edge of their world—the shape of a woman lying on her back, her long hair streaming behind her. Her breasts pointing to the sky, knees raised. Plain as day, once you'd been shown.

Aaron pointed between a Tudor and a Colonial. "That's where the barn was," he said. "Right about there."

Janice shaded her eyes from the unaccustomed sun and looked down. She tried to remember the barn in the midst of its rolling fields. She'd lived in Van Luykensville all of her life and surely she'd seen it. But she'd been a child, really, when the lightning struck. She tried to imagine it as Aaron had described it to her, just now: a brilliant thing, a manifestation of pure light. She put a hand on Aaron's back. It felt strange to touch him. She'd always been afraid, really, to even look at him too closely. How stupid, she thought. How childish. She ran her hand down his spine. "Who bought the land? After, you know, your father and all."

Aaron leaned back against the warmth of her palm and closed his eyes. "Some rich city guys. A conglomerate. They planned a golf course. But it never happened. They gave my mother about one-tenth what the land was worth and then they just let it rot. Lying fallow for years, until just recently, when they sold it for millions to these developers. Right away, though, back then, they tore down the farmhouse and then they just let it lie there, a pile of rubble that they just pushed into its own foundation." He willed her hand to continue rubbing. He knew he was playing up the story, just a bit, for sympathy value, but what the hell. A guy like him, he'd never turn down the chance of a mercy fuck, not in this lifetime, he wouldn't. "When I got out of the hospital—I stayed there six months, while my mother sold the house, packed and moved, all of that—I still couldn't walk and had bandages over most of my face. So Peter pulled me, in his wagon, I swear, all the way over here and down to the old house. We went through the rubble. I found four of my Star Wars guys that my mom had forgotten to pack. It was a kind of triumph. Peter found one of my dad's old Playboys. That was pretty cool, too." He turned and looked straight into Janice's eyes, letting her see his ravaged face. Her skin glowed a soft green in his vision. "Naked ladies. The very thing, Peter said, to bring a guy back to the land of the living, when he'd been traversing the halls of the dead and the half-dead, struck down by God's own hand, a bolt of blue out of the heavens themselves. Peter really talked like that, even then. I can still hear him say it: *the very thing.*" He tilted his head, asking her the question: "Might still work, right? You think?"

Janice looked into his eyes: the right blue, the left a kind of glazed, shimmery silver. She looked at the houses behind him and the mountains, far off behind the houses. The Hudson River lay between the land and the mountains, but you couldn't see it. Some things in life were like that: the river that had created this land, shaped and carved the whole valley, was the one thing you couldn't really see. Not from here, anyway. Janice cupped one hand around Aaron's wounded cheek and she brought her lips against his. It felt odd, at first, one half of the mouth so still, the other half so mobile and so warm, so searching of her own.

They moved only a little ways, into the long grass at the edge of the woods. Aaron's clothes only came halfway off, but Janice stood up for him, taking her things off one at a time, letting him look, letting him have his fill of looking. She wasn't what she'd once been—her breasts were fallen and her hips wide—but still. Maybe Aaron's skewed vision would put these things right.

When she lay down on her back beside him, Aaron felt as if the mountains themselves had come to life and come to him: woman on her back, knees raised. He took her left breast in his good right hand and he swung his hips over hers, easily, easily. It was all so much simpler than he could have imagined. She touched him everywhere and he didn't have the heart to tell her that he couldn't feel her fingers on his left side: that his left nipple had no sensation, that even his left ball was without a hint of thrill. It was enough that she was willing to touch him. More than enough.

As for Janice, she had tried to imagine what it would be like—even when she'd been a girl, lying beneath some long-haired teenage boy, she'd wondered. She'd imagined that from Aaron's left side, a kind of magic flowed. That, somehow, the lightning's power still lingered in his flesh. That when her skin came in contact with any of those parts of him that had been filled with pure electricity, the voltage would run, flashing and glimmering along her every nerve ending. That when she came, her back would filament into a perfect arc of current and that, afterward, she would cry like a newborn babe.

It wasn't like that, of course. It was awkward. It was difficult. She had to keep shifting her hips to accommodate his off-center thrusts. The grass was wet and cold beneath her. The left side of his body rested on her right side as dead weight. Still, still. When she decided to reverse the procedure, take things into her own hands, so to speak, when she got on top, the sun warmed her back and ass in little patches. The sun was hot, steamy with all of the withheld warmth of this misshapen June. It felt wonderful on her skin. And she could look down into those mismatched eyes and see gratitude in the right and wonder in the left. She watched, carefully, as Aaron came, his voice rising like a little boy's. She didn't think she would, but sometimes, you're just not in control, no matter what you think. Because exactly as she was thinking that there was no way it was going to happen, her body opened like a flower and she came, and came, and came, raining down. Raining sweetly down.

MRS. VAN ALLEN, NAPPING, cried out in her sleep: *We're going.* And the houses on Incubator Lane shifted just a little bit more.

PETER JOHNSON, HALF-NAPPING, half-dreamed of Harriet Burget, dead at fifty-one, just a year after the passing of her daughter Harriet A., at the age of fifteen, and just six years after the passing of her other daughter, Rachel M., at the age of eighteen months and twenty-six days. Harriet Burget's gravestone said *Suffer the children to come unto me.* Rachel M.'s said *We'll Meet Again.* In his floating state, Peter took Harriet's hand—a skeleton's hand—and he lifted her from the flood waters. But she pulled away from his grasp. "Not without the children, Mr. Johnson," she said. "I can't be going without my girls." And so he had to leave her there, in the end, when he could no longer stand and had to stretch out his arms and swim.

RIGHT AFTER A BLOODY red sunset, the rain started up again. At first only light spatters, then curtains of water teeming down.

AARON DIDN'T BOTHER to check the cellar. Instead, he slept soundly in his bed. He could still smell Janice's scent on his skin.

Janice went to work as she always did, covering the night shift at the Stewarts shop up the road. But the other girl laughed at her, said Janice was so spacy and smiley that she must be stoned. They all thought that Janice lived a sad life. But they also all thought that Janice had interesting secrets—she always looked like she might. Janice shook her head at the girl and said, no, that wasn't it, that wasn't it, at all. She went into the tiny bathroom at the back of the store and looked at her face in the mirror: Her eyes did not look stoned, not really. Only softened, somehow. Gentled.

Mrs. Van Allen wasn't sleepy, so she sat up in bed, took her weight on her arms, and slung her butt into her chair. Through the wheels, she felt it: a sudden wrench, a loosening of the grip of the land. The giving up, the giving out. She cried out, but there was no one home to hear her.

The jolt woke Peter. He tried to get out of bed and it was then that he realized that the floor was tilted. He adjusted his weight and stood, unevenly. It came to him that this was how Aaron must always feel, off balance. The house shifted. Aaron. Peter made his way to his kitchen door, holding to the walls and cursing. When he'd gotten the door open, he bellowed: "Wake up, bro. It's time."

Into Aaron's dreams came a vague noise: just a whisper, really. Just the touch of a hand on his cheek, trying to wake him. His mother's gentle hand. He preferred, really, not to wake. But something called him. He sat up. His bed was tiptoeing across the floor.

PETER REACHED AARON'S DOOR at exactly the same moment that Aaron did. They stared at each other, the driveway bucking beneath their bare feet. Peter, suddenly, started to laugh. "Praise be," he shouted. "It's apocalypse *now*."

Aaron looked across the street, seeing it through sheets of green rain. He shouted back at Peter. "Mrs. Van Allen—we have to get her out."

Peter, too, looked over.

The front door of number 6 opened and the wheelchair rolled out. Mrs. Van Allen, her hair white and wild as a phantom's, had made it as far as the porch.

Aaron and Peter began to move toward her. But Aaron was so slow that Peter got to her much more quickly. He took her right out of her chair and lifted her in his arms. With a mighty grunt, he centered her against his chest, cradled like a sleeping baby. He carried her up the slope of her yard, away from the house, step by step. Rain sheeted off his broad back and he crooned to her the whole time: *Sleep sweet babe, you art at rest; no cloud of sorrow shades thy breast*. By the time Aaron reached them, the old lady was awash in rain, but safely propped against a tree, Peter's enormous t-shirt wrapped around her shoulders. The ground up here seemed stable. Below them, numbers 3 and 5 were quivering like baby birds balanced on the edge of a nest.

AT STEWARTS, SOMETHING SHOT through Janice; seventh daughter of a seventh daughter, she had these moments. This one pierced her chest, a sword-point of fear. She took off through the door, running. She slammed herself into her car. Its headlights lit only a small tunnel in the teeming darkness but it was wide enough to see her home.

PETER WAS RUBBING a hand across his bare chest. He massaged his left arm. His breathing was ragged. He looked at Aaron. He smiled. "I'm going to see to the graves," he said.

Aaron grabbed his arm. "Shit, no. That's crazy."

Peter put a massive hand on Aaron's head. *"With a doleful grace bid the world adieu.* That's from Sylvestes's stone. For once in my life, let me have grace, okay?" He turned and lumbered away. As he disappeared into the rain, his voice came back: *"AMF YO YO, bro. AMF YO YO."*

JANICE FOUND HER mother and Aaron sitting together at the top of what had been a small hill behind her house. Now it was the jagged edge of a cliff. The houses, all three of them, were simply gone. The street itself, gone. The mud was still sliding, sinuous as snakes. Rocks still clamored and spun. The noise was incredible, as if the very earth were screaming. The air smelled of dirt and rot and old, old bones. The rain poured down and lightning blued the sky.

Cabbage Night

WE DIDN'T MEAN TO, not really.

Or maybe we did. It's hard to say. The three of us—Pearl, Ruby and Opal (that is, me)—were just little girls in January 1954 when Ernest Elheim, the man next door, died suddenly. Well, I was a little girl. Four years old, a mere mite. But Pearl was not quite a child. Pearl was twelve and had been kissed. Maybe that had something to do with how it all turned out. Ruby was nine. Had she been kissed? Would we have even known? She wouldn't have said. She didn't say much, then or ever. Ruby was, and is, beyond me.

Fifty-five years later, there is only me. Pearl is dead. Cardiac failure. Her chest was cracked open like an egg, her bare heart massaged and shocked and pummeled, all to no avail. And Ruby is gone—where, we never really heard. She simply called a cab and disappeared, more than thirty years ago. Just up and left her apartment one fine day, totally disappeared. Poof, into the ether. Call her Amelia Earhart, she's that far gone. Or perhaps not completely gone—and that may be worse.

But as far as I know, it's just me left. Last one standing. Go ahead, call me Ishmael.

Here's the tale I'm bound to repeat, over and over again.

IN THE LATE FALL of 1953, we three girls decided that the man next door was a monster and must be destroyed. The matter of exactly why is puzzling, today, some half-century later. At the time, it was obvious: Ernest Elheim was sucking our mother's lifeblood away, day by day. As the nights grew longer and the air grew colder, our mother was leaving us, drop by crimson drop. Something had to be done. And so we did it.

In order by age, we girls were called Pearl, Ruby and Opal. Obviously, our mother was overly fanciful and/or downright silly. Did she really think her girls—plain-faced, mousy-haired, skinny-assed girls—were jewels? Certainly, our mother could not have understood the daily struggles of gem-named children in the rough streets of whatever New Jersey town we found ourselves in. Wherever our father, who was scrabbling up the corporate ladder at a cable manufacturing company, was transferred. A new town nearly every year. Where our names were put to good use by neighborhood wits: *Here come Puke, Ratty and Awful. Putrid, Rank and Ooze.* Et cetera. Pearl, at twelve, was beginning to care what the boys yelled at her. Somewhere in her still-flat chest, nasty words stuck like arrows. Ruby, nine, didn't even seem to notice. And I, at four, found most words funny. I would giggle when the big boys—and sometimes the girls—yelled. And then Pearl would have to pinch me, hard, to make me stop. Once begun, I've always had trouble stopping.

There was one particular incident involving Pearl and a boy. Call him Kendall Johannson; in any case, picture a popular, blond-haired, smiler of a boy. You know the type: that one may smile, and smile, and be a villain. That September, Kendall started passing notes all around the sixth grade, telling everyone he was in love with the new girl. In the notes, he called her Pretty Pearl. One afternoon, in sight of nearly everyone on the playground, Pearl let him kiss her. Deeply, sweetly, opening her virgin lips to taste his sharp tongue. She fell in love, of course, with the savor of his mouth. But, alas, the next morning, his villainy became manifest: Kendall and his friends lined up along the fence as Pearl and Ruby—I was too young yet for school—entered the school yard. Pearl was already smiling, shyly and happily, when Kendall began the boys' new chant: *Stupid slut, Oyster shit, Looks like crap and smells like it.* Ruby, unfortunately, laughed. Presumably, Ruby was tickled by the "oyster shit" bit, since really, what else is a pearl? In any case, Pearl had nowhere to turn, in that awful moment of humiliation, for sisterly comfort, and that nowhere-ness twisted something inside her. Right then, I believe, Pearl's heart, though it kept beating for forty more years, broke.

If only we could have stayed inside our house, whichever of the identical ranch houses was ours for the year, things might have been fine. Inside, oh inside, we lived in our made-up worlds, where we truly were gems, where Pearl glowed milky white, Ruby deep scarlet, and Opal smoky blue. Inside, we were valiant and pure and truly loved. Inside, our mother baked and sang while she cleaned. Our mother braided our hair and read to us. And in June of 1953, that particular house was fresh and new; we always moved in June, right after school ended in our old town, to give us girls the summer to settle into the new. That June, our mother read all of our favorites: *The Wind in the Willows, The House at Pooh Corner, The Five Little Peppers and How They Grew, Anne of Green Gables, Lad: A Dog, Heidi.* But by September, our mother's selections inexplicably deepened and darkened. Our mother's voice took on gravel as she read us the brothers Grimm, *Tales from the*

Arabian Nights, and strange, adult things. I remember their titles, even yet: "A Narrative of the Captivity and Restoration of Mrs. Mary Rowlandson," "Upon a Spider Catching a Fly," "Because I Could Not Stop for death." Of course, of course: "he kindly stopped for me." Terrible, wonderful stuff, forever implanted in my brain. I can still recite that spider poem, or bits of it, and often do, when in my cups: "Whereas the silly Fly,/ Caught by its leg/ Thou by the throate tookst hastily./ And 'hinde the head/ Bite Dead."

By October, our mother had stopped reading altogether. She stopped baking and stopped, it seemed, loving us at all. She kept sending us outside to play, all the time. *Go on,* she'd say. *Now. You're making me nauseous.* And, perhaps it was true that we had actually become sickening, because our mother also kept running to the toilet to throw up. That fall, Mother slapped Ruby when she spilled her grape juice on the couch. Then there were two blue stains: the blotch on the couch and the bruise on Ruby's cheekbone. Mother sent us outside without jackets; she forgot what Pearl and Ruby liked in their school lunches and gave them slimy bologna every day. Then she stopped making lunches and dinners entirely and when our father came home from work, the table was bare and the kitchen cold. There was yelling in the house and, after a while, our father didn't come home at all. There was no solemn family talk about this, no reassurance that Father would always love us. No, no—in those days, children were not consulted or informed about their parents' lives. Children knew what they could figure out and that was all. If we got it wrong, so be it. *Que sera, sera.*

Mother got worse. She rarely left her bedroom. On school days, when my sisters were gone, she let me wander the streets alone, nose running and chin chapped. And I was just a baby, really. Wandering and warbling to myself, sticky little spider songs.

That fall, it became clear, Mother was possessed. Pearl whispered the word in our ears, long sibilant whispers: *She's possessed.* And Pearl knew exactly who was to blame. Ernest Elheim. The man next door. The man with thick black hair (our father was comfortingly bald), a wide smile (way too many teeth), and an invisible war wound. A wound so bad that he didn't even go to work, like all the other men in New Jersey. Instead, his *wife* worked. And the Elheims had no children. Not a one. The house next door represented, to us three girls, an upheaval of the natural order of things. No wonder that house bred monsters: how could it not?

When pressed about the nature of Mr. Elheim's mysterious malady, our mother only said *Korea*, a word that made me smile, at first. Ernest Elheim had been hurt in his *Korea*. When Pearl—twelve-year-olds sometimes push their mothers—asked how, exactly, Mr. Elheim had been hurt, and where, exactly, on his body the wound was located, and why, exactly, the man couldn't go to work, Mother told her to shut the hell up. Mother turned away.

But Pearl knew the real story and that night she sat me and Ruby down on her bed and told us. Pearl used her scary-story voice, deep and resonant: *In the faraway land of Korea, there are birds who eat hearts. These birds fly at night. Their feathers are jet black, so you cannot see them. Their wings are silent, so you cannot hear them. They can fly through glass and screens and even walls, so you cannot keep them out of your room, no matter how you try. When you are sleeping, you must not lie on your back, unless you lock your hands over your chest. If you forget to lock your hands or if your fingers come apart in your sleep, the Korean heart-suckers will*

*see you. Their eyes are very good in the dark. They will land softly
with their gentle, feathery feet on your belly. Even if you wake up,
then, and clasp your fingers tight and cry out, it is already too late.
The big black birds have already put their razor beaks—peck!—right
between your ribs. They have already lifted out your bloody, beating
heart and they have already set in its place a black egg. They will
fly silently away. They will carry your heart to their nest and feed it
to their hungry babies. When you go back to sleep, thinking it was
only a dream, the black shell will crack inside your chest and out
will crawl a wet, slimy chick. The chick will, forever after, beat its
wings in your chest. It will feel like your heart going hup tup, hup
tup but it is not. It is the black bird who poisons your blood with
badness. Someday, the bird will break out of the cage of your chest.
You will bleed black blood and die. Then the bird will go back out
into the night, to land on another victim. But until then, it stays
inside, beating and beating its angry wings. And you are, forever
after, very evil. You look human but you are a monster. And a danger
to your community.*

Ruby and I were quiet for some time after Pearl told us this.
And then I—who was a very bright four-year-old, very articulate
and curious—asked, "Is it catching? Can the bird-heart person
give it to someone else?"

Pearl poked me. She went on in her story voice. *Yes, indeed.
The evil bird-heart person can put a black egg into another person.*

I said, "How?"

Pearl shrugged, looking wise and old. *He can spit an egg
into someone else's mouth. A tiny egg. No bigger than a poppy-seed.
But inside, it grows. And it drinks the person's blood, drop by drop.*

I said, "Oh. Is that what happened to Mommy?"

Yes. The tiny black egg is growing in her, right now. Mr. Elheim put it in her mouth, with his lips and his tongue. I saw him. It's in there, all right.

I said, "Can we get it out?"

Pearl thought, for a minute. *Maybe.*

Then I said, "How?"

We will have to kill him.

WELL, WELL, WELL. Today, of course, it seems unlikely that we actually did manage to kill Mr. Elheim. But die he did. And, afterward, Mother did recover, partly. She started cooking again and Father came back and most of the yelling stopped. But the baby brother born the next summer did look suspiciously beaky and he had feathery black hair. He was tiny—under five pounds—and he did not cry properly. No, he gave out little indignant squawks, instead of good, lusty cries. We girls could never trust him, ever. Interloper. We never counted him as one as our own—not then and not now, either. Changeling.

Who's to say what causes what? Who's to say why anyone dies, suddenly? How can we ever separate magic from mundane? It's impossible to judge. But *something* was put into motion that fall. That's beyond dispute.

★ ★ ★

OUR PLAN, AT FIRST, was simple: while Pearl and Ruby were at school, I would wait and watch. When the Monster appeared, I would follow him and I would then report to my sisters on what he was up to, in detail. I was small and unattractive—that's exactly what they told me, poor thing!—and not likely to be noticed. I would be the perfect spy.

And as it turned out, I was. The very next day, when I was cast out of the house by my mother, sent sweaterless into late October's biting wind and the flailing, failing, falling leaves of many oaks, I saw the Monster come out of his own back door and walk into our backyard. So I simply went back inside—oh-so-quietly, quick, quick, quick—using the front door, and I sat—oh-so-silent, oh-so-still—in the closet in the front hall. And, in no time at all, the Monster swept in through the back door and straight up to the bedroom where Mother lay sleeping (or weeping). He didn't knock. He went inside the room, closing the door behind him. I—clever little sneak—crept up the staircase and curled myself outside the bedroom door. My mother's voice was low. The Monster seemed not to speak at all. If he had, I reasoned, his voice would be a terrible croaking caw, the black bird clinging to his throat, its egg at the ready. But then Mother began to gasp—*o, o, o*—and then to moan—*ooh, ooh, ooh*—and, in a few minutes, to yell, high-pitched and desperate—*shit, shit, SHIT.* I shivered. And then, in another minute, a thick, scraping Monster voice: *Ahhhhh.* And then my mother's quavering sobs.

I scuttled away, flew out into the wind and into the sharp-edged leaves. My face, I'm sure, was the color of ash. Even the cold could not redden those chalky cheeks. As if I myself—poor mite—had been drained of every last drop of blood.

BUT I—A RESILIENT CHILD—soon recovered. That night, I told the tale to my sisters, in great detail, in the darkness of Pearl's bed. I was quite the little actress: I imitated the gasps—*o,o,o.* I mimicked the moans—*ooh, ooh, ooh.* I took great glee in shouting the forbidden yells—*shit, shit, SHIT.* But when it came time to reproduce that monstrous, deep, long *Ahhhhh*, I couldn't quite get it right. I didn't have the throat for it. But I did my best.

And Pearl, at least, got it. Ruby, who could tell? She listened—Ruby always listened—but she also kept stroking her cat, Mr. Mouse, all gray and nearly invisible in the dim light. Pearl cleared her throat. She pondered. Then she pronounced: *He must be destroyed.*

Ruby and I nodded. That was obvious. But how, I asked.

And Pearl drummed her fingers on the bedspread—lumpy green chenille—and thought. *There is only one way. On Cabbage Night, we must burn three things: an item of the Monster's clothing, a piece of our mother's hair, and one black feather. When these three items are consumed, the Monster's strength will fail and the seed he has planted in our mother will wither away and die.*

I put my head down on Ruby's pillow—we three girls were all sleeping in the same bed these days, what did our mother care, anyway?—and put my thumb in my mouth. Of course I did. I was afraid of what was coming. I had a feeling I'd done my spycraft too well.

And, yes, exactly as I feared, Pearl gave me the hardest task: the next time the Monster was in Mother's room, I must sneak in—quiet as a snake, soft as a lamb—and get some bit of the Monster's clothes. A button, a shoelace, anything. Pearl said that the Monster would shed his clothes in Mother's room and so something would be at hand for my thieving.

Pearl could, quite easily, gather strands of Mother's hair—as mousy brown as our own—from her brush. And Ruby? Oh, Ruby kept all sorts of precious bits and pieces in a shoebox under the bed—rocks, animal bones, tangles of string, beetles, butterfly wings, Oreos, and feathers. Surely, Pearl suggested, one of those feathers was black. Ruby spoke, for the first time. "No black ones. I'll dip one in ink."

Pearl scoffed. "Ink? Who the fuck has ink?" In just the last month, Pearl had started to talk this way, as if Kendall Johannson's perfidious kiss had coarsened her tongue. "Just go out and find a black feather, you jerk. They're everywhere."

Ruby nodded and pulled Mr. Mouse under the covers with her. His kneading and purring kept me awake and that was why I noticed, late late late in the night, that Pearl's hand had crept between Pearl's skinny thighs and that Pearl was making tiny little sounds: *o, o, o*. Pearl's skinny hips were lifting off the mattress. I closed my ears, tight. I went to sleep, steeled in my resolve: we *must* kill the Monster. On Cabbage Night. For so it was decreed.

[PERHAPS I SHOULD pause the tale here to explain Cabbage Night to anyone who did not grow up in New Jersey, in that faraway, long ago time. It's nearly impossible, nowadays, to understand the liberties afforded children back then on October 30, the day before Halloween, every year. Nowadays, all of those children, the little monsters, would be arrested for vandalism and criminal mischief—indeed, in some parts of the country, this night was called Mischief Night, a far less interesting title. Nowadays, parents would be hauled into court for contributing to the delinquency of minors. But in those days, parents bent before the wind of ancient impulse and let their children out into a night designed for mayhem. Some even bought dozens of eggs, especially. A few examples of Cabbage Night tricks: thrown eggs. Dog shit placed in paper bags and set afire on front porches; the house owner— usually the father—furiously stomped out the flames, splattering shit far and wide. Pillowcases filled with flour, then swung wide and hard, knocking younger children sprawling, whitening their faces and clothes, leaving behind whole troops of small stunned ghosts. Smashing mailboxes with hockey sticks, croquet mallets and baseball bats. Much, much running and shrieking through the streets. *Lord of the Flies,* for one glorious night.]

So. On October 29, I waited until the Monster was inside Mother's room. I sat outside the door, dressed by my own hands in overalls too big and a striped t-shirt too small. Barefoot—there were no clean socks—and quite dirty. There had been no baths for a month. I was sucking my thumb. Until that fall, I'd broken this babyish habit. But, right then, I needed it. The sounds, this time, weren't the same. Indeed, there was no sound at all from Mother. That silence was terrible. Maybe my mother, right here, right now, was dying. Or dead. I stood up, on wobbly legs, and put my hand on the doorknob. I leaned my head against the thin wood of the door and listened. A new series of sounds emerged: deep, ugly grunts in Monster tones. *Hunh, hunh, hunh.*

I—oh, child—opened the door.

The Monster was lying on his back on the bed. He was wearing a shirt—blue—and one sock—black. His body was covered with black hairs, curling. His head was thrown back and he was grunting. It was very loud in the room: *HUNH. HUNH. HUNH.* His eyes were closed. His hands were pressing my mother's head to his crotch, his fingers knotted in her hair.

My mother was licking. My mother was sucking. Then my mother was gagging.

My heart wanted to stop, it really did. It tried to end

everything, right then, right there. But hearts are, after all, terribly strong. It kept right on beating.

With one long *HUUNH*, the Monster's eyes came open. They saw me there, thumb in mouth, and they flamed. The Monster's lips tried to form a word but there was no sound. Only fury, on his mouth.

I bent down and grabbed one black sock from the floor. I held it—smelly, nasty thing—to my chest and backed up, out of the room, silent and quick.

Mother never saw me. I closed the door as quietly as a ghost and I ran to my room. I did not hear the final *HUUUUNH* and I did not see Mother swallow the seed. I did not. I swear that I did not.

OCTOBER 30. THE DAY has darkened and become Cabbage Night. We three girls have gone out into the howling, wild dark. What does our mother care? Our mother is locked in her room, crying.

Pearl has brought a brown tangle of hair. Pearl also carries a bag of charcoal and a can of lighter fluid and matches. Pearl is prepared. Although I have not told my sisters the story of how I obtained it—I cannot, I cannot—I have a stinky black sock. And Ruby has something in a cage.

We hunker down in the furthest corner of our backyard. The grass has grown wild and long. It is thick with fallen leaves. The bare branches of the trees toss above our heads. The night is alive with the screams and shrieking laughter of children set free, to be bad. Let out on purpose, to be bad.

Pearl piles the charcoal in a neat black heap. She sets on top of it the little nest of mother's hair. She gestures to me: *The Monster's clothing,* she intones.

I drop the sock onto the charcoal. I move back and squat, wiping my hands on my pants, over and over again, before I put my thumb in my mouth.

Pearl looks up, impatient. *Where is the black feather?*

Ruby steps forward. She has Mr. Mouse's carrier in her arms. She sets it down. Inside, the girls can see the glow of the cat's green eyes but nothing of the cat himself.

Pearl frowns. "What the fuck is this?" Her intonation has slipped and she sounds just like a twelve-year-old girl. She tries again: *Sister, why have you not brought the black feather? Why is this feline here?*

Ruby holds up one hand. Out of the deep pocket of her skirt, she draws out a bird. Not just a feather—a whole bird. It is black. And it is alive, barely. Both of its wings seem broken—they flap uselessly. It cheeps, its beak wide and pleading.

Pearl and I hold our breath. Somehow, Ruby has gotten beyond us. She is changing the rules of the game. Raising the stakes. Upping the ante.

Ruby holds the wounded bird above her head and chants, into the wind, into the dark, into the night: *Oh Gods of Cabbage, accept this gift. Honor our sacrifice. Grant our plea. Kill the Monster Man.* The bird flutters. It struggles in Ruby's hand. It tries, weakly, to peck her fingers. But the hand is firm, unrelenting. Ruby opens the little metal door of the cat carrier and thrusts the bird inside. There is a good deal of useless fluttering and panicked twittering. Broken wings agitate the air in the cramped dark space. The cat backs up, surprised. Then it creeps forward, delighted. There is a deep growl in the cat's throat. Then a spring. Biting, clawing, tossing. There is blood. And feathers. Plenty of sticky black feathers. It all takes a long time. Pearl and I are shivering.

Ruby smiles.

The cat munches his treat. When he is done, he sits back and licks his bloody paws, his fastidious, delicate tongue moving between toes. Ruby reaches into the mess and takes three feathers in her fingers. She adds them to the pile of charcoal. She nods to Pearl, who saturates the whole thing with fluid. One strike of a match and it explodes into bright orange flame.

I try to step away, but Ruby has my hand. Ruby has Pearl's hand, too, and so we all stand before the fire, together, bound by what we have done.

Perhaps if we had turned around, we would have seen our mother standing in the window of her bedroom, shaking, wrapped in a blanket from her smelly, sticky bed.

And what might Mother see? Mother sees three skinny girls, their stringy, filthy hair lifting in the wind. Mother sees a brilliant fire and her three girls, dark silhouettes holding hands. They look very small against that lurid light. They look lost. No, worse, they look forsaken. Abandoned. They look like orphans.

HAVE PATIENCE: THERE isn't much more to tell. By the first month of the New Year, January 1954, Ernest Elheim was dead. The cause of death, whispered around the neighborhood, was odd but certainly not supernatural: a piece of Korean shrapnel, lodged in the muscles of his back for oh-so-many months, moved. It made its sharp way into his chest and punctured a lung. Ernest Elheim died in his bed, lying on his back, gasping and choking, blood bubbling from his lips: *aaa, aaa, aaa.*

Pearl, Ruby and I—mere children, unimportant—did not attend Mr. Elheim's funeral.

But our mother and our father went. They went together to the church and to the Elheims' house, afterward. Our mother brought a lemon pound cake to Mr. Elheim's wife. I imagine that Mother pulled the grieving woman into her arms and held her there, against her swelling belly. I am sure that our mother murmured soft shushing sounds to the widow, soothing and comforting her: *You poor girl. There there. There there.*

Hollis Seamon is the author of a mystery novel, *Flesh;* a young adult novel, *Somebody Up There HATES You* (forthcoming, Algonquin Books); and a previous short story collection, *Body Work.* She has published short stories in many journals, including *Bellevue Literary Review, Greensboro Review, Fiction International, Chicago Review, Nebraska Review, Persimmon Tree,* and *Calyx.* Her work has been anthologized in  *The Strange History of Suzanne LaFleshe and Other Stories of Women and Fatness, A Line of Cutting Women, The Best of the Bellevue Literary Review,* and *Sacred Ground.* She is a recipient of a fiction fellowship from the New York Foundation for the Arts. Seamon is Professor of English at the College of Saint Rose in Albany NY and also teaches for the MFA in Creative Writing Program at Fairfield University, Fairfield CT. She lives in Kinderhook NY.

OTHER BOOKS FROM ABLE MUSE PRESS

Ben Berman, *Strange Borderlands - Poems*

Michael Cantor, *Life in the Second Circle - Poems*

Catherine Chandler, *Lines of Flight - Poems*

Margaret Ann Griffiths, *Grasshopper - The Poetry of M A Griffiths*

April Lindner, *This Bed Our Bodies Shaped - Poems*

Alexander Pepple (Editor), *Able Muse Anthology*

Alexander Pepple (Editor), *Able Muse - a review of poetry, prose & art*
  (semiannual issues, Winter 2010 onward)

James Pollock, *Sailing to Babylon - Poems*

Aaron Poochigian, *The Cosmic Purr - Poems*

Matthew Buckley Smith, *Dirge for an Imaginary World - Poems*

Wendy Videlock, *The Dark Gnu and Other Poems*

Wendy Videlock, *Nevertheless - Poems*

Richard Wakefield, *A Vertical Mile - Poems*

www.ablemusepress.com

CPSIA information can be obtained at www.ICGtesting.com
Printed in the USA
LVOW121547100413

328560LV00014B/1330/P